Longarm's mouth felt dry as he watched the ragged line of fifty-odd masked men advancing at a slow but steady pace.

A Minute Man standing close with a sawed-off, double-barrel ten-guage called out, "You know what we're here for, Longarm. We want the murderous half-wit who murdered Mildred Powell. We don't want no judge saying you can't hang mean kids!"

Longarm replied, "How many times were you planning on hanging a prisoner on the same charge, with no warrant and no trial?"

Another voice called, "Hand him over. Now. Unless you was planning on doing the rope dance beside him . . ."

DON'T MISS THESE
ALL-ACTION WESTERN SERIES
FROM THE BERKLEY PUBLISHING GROUP

TABOR EVANS

LONGARM

AND THE MINUTE MEN

J

JOVE BOOKS, NEW YORK

LONGARM AND THE MINUTE MEN

A Jove Book / published by arrangement with
the author

PRINTING HISTORY
Jove edition / September 1996

The Putnam Berkley World Wide Web site address is
http://www.berkley.com

ISBN: 0-515-11942-3

A JOVE BOOK®
Jove Books are published by The Berkley Publishing Group,
200 Madison Avenue, New York, New York 10016.
JOVE and the "J" design are trademarks
belonging to Jove Publications, Inc.

PRINTED IN THE UNITED STATES OF AMERICA

10 9 8 7 6 5 4 3 2 1

AND THE
MINUTE MEN

Chapter 1

It was going for midnight and the dark jailhouse windows were staring out at the empty courthouse square like the eye sockets of a moonlit skull.

One of the county lawmen inside lit yet another smoke before he muttered, "The night winds have died and it feels as if the whole durned town is holding its breath out yonder."

The sheriff replied, "I'm afraid it is. I reckon we'd best sneak them prisoners out the back about now. We can all mount up and ride gentle when the church bell across the way tolls twelve to muffle our hoofbeats a mite."

All three of his deputies made as if to follow their boss back to the patent cells, but he soberly said, "Just Clancy here. I want the rest of you to cover out front as Clancy and me move Bubblehead and that federal warrant out to the stable. I'll send word when it's time for the bunch of us to light out for the Rocking Seven."

Suiting actions to his words, the lanky gray sheriff led the more well-fed Deputy Clancy into the back, where a single wall sconce cast feeble light and ominous shadows through the bars and across the two prisoners.

1

The sheriff unlocked the cell door of Dancing Dave Loman first, saying, "It's time to drop your cocks and grab your socks, boys. We may have visitors most any time now. You and young Bubblehead will enjoy their visit more if you ain't here."

The tall, brawny train robber was already wearing his socks. As he sat on the edge of his bunk, hauling on his boots, he asked in a worried tone, "Necktie party? I just got here and I've never wronged a soul in this Sand Hill Country, for Chrissake!"

The sheriff said, "Hurry it up. They describe themselves as the Minute Men and I don't know how many minutes we have to work with! They're almost certain to come for that *other* guest of the county tonight! So let's see some of that famous dancing, Dancing Dave!"

Then he was unlocking the cell next door to call more loudly, in a weary tone, "Wake up and rub the sleep out of your slanty eyes, you poor dumb bastard! Didn't you hear us tell you we'd be riding out to the Rocking Seven tonight?"

The short, dumpy, and awkwardly moving Bubblehead Burnside rolled off his own bunk in an oddly graceful if tottering way, and grinned childishly up at the sheriff, replying, "Aw, I wasn't sleeping. I been waiting and waiting to go for that pony ride. I *like* to ride ponies. Don't you?"

The far taller train robber joined them, guarded casually by Deputy Clancy, and stared uncertainly at his fellow prisoner. He saw now why the kid's attempts at neighborly conversation that evening had sounded so odd. Loman had already heard that they called the towheaded kid in the other cell Bubblehead. He'd had no idea the nickname could fit anyone so well. As Bubblehead Burnside joined them in the corridor, the train robber quietly asked Deputy Clancy, "What's wrong with him? Has he lost all his marbles?"

Bubblehead heard and, even though he hadn't been asked the question, answered it. "I ain't lost my marbles, mister. I

2

got me a whole mason jar full of marbles. *Almost* a whole jar, I bet. My big sister, Rose, is watching them for me at our house. They don't allow no marble playing here in *this* house. I don't know why. Do you?''

The sheriff said, ''Be still, Bubblehead. Clancy, douse that wall light so's I can crack the back door and see if the coast is clear.''

''We're going for a pony ride,'' Bubblehead confided to his fellow prisoner.

To which Dancing Dave Loman could only reply, ''Jesus H. Christ, I was *complimenting* him when I took him for a half-wit!''

There was a moment of total darkness as Clancy doused the dim wall sconce. Bubblehead whimpered, ''I don't like it in here!''

Then the sheriff opened the back door to spill a slowly widening stripe of moonlight across the concrete floor as Bubblehead laughed like a little kid and asked, ''Can we go out and play now? I like to go out and play at night when the moon is shining. It ain't too dark when the moon is shining. I like the moon. It's pretty.''

The sheriff told him to be still and follow after him. But Bubblehead babbled on as they moved across the stable yard in single file, and Dancing Dave turned to Deputy Clancy behind him. ''You say night riders might be coming for your village idiot? What did he do to them, steal some of their marbles?''

Clancy quietly replied, ''Raped a lady. Then he stabbed her dead.''

Dancing Dave protested, ''This harmless-looking half-wit? It's hard to picture him knowing why boys and girls are built different! Are you sure it was him? Who said it was him?''

Clancy softly answered, ''Her. The gal made a dying declaration to the ones as came running when they heard her screaming from the church. He'd cut her bad afore he run off, but he hadn't had the sense to make certain she was

3

dead. She was the church lady as taught Sunday school over to First Calvinist. So she'd been letting him sit in with the little kids, never dreaming that he was lusting for her body all the time she thought she was leading him *away* from temptation!''

By this time the sheriff, in the lead, had made it to the stable door. As he opened it, a quartet of figures, wearing feed sacks over their heads and shoulders, stepped out into the moonlight with drawn guns.

Things got mighty quiet for a spell. Then the sheriff cleared his throat and said, ''You don't need to be so harsh, boys. Our prosecuting attorney is willing to bet a month's pay that Bubblehead will hang for the murder of Miss Mildred Powell, and we've been holding this other cuss on a federal warrant!''

A very heavy masked man with a ten-gauge Greener aimed downright rude replied in an icy tone, ''We don't want to *bet* on that hanging, Sheriff. Miss Mildred had a lot of friends in these parts, and the way she lost her virginity was mighty damned harsh as well. So step aside and let us have 'em, unless you'd care to *join* 'em, over by the spot we've picked out to string 'em up!''

''I want to go home now,'' Bubblehead Burnside whimpered. But then other masked men were pouring out of the stable as the sheriff said, ''All right, I can't stop you from taking the half-wit, but this other prisoner was picked up on a federal warrant and there's this U.S. deputy marshal on his way up from Denver for him, hear?''

It might have worked. But another member of the bunch called out in a worried tone, ''Let the federal want be, Porky. They never said they wanted us to take anybody but Bubblehead, and where's the call for us to hang a total stranger?''

The burly leader called Porky snorted in disgust and replied, ''You just now *called* it, you asshole.''

Swinging the twin muzzles of his Greener so the sheriff could stare straight into them, Porky quietly said, ''*You* didn't hear anybody here identify any of us by name, did you, Sheriff?''

To which the older and wiser man could only reply, ''I wasn't paying attention, mister. You say somebody called someone here by name?''

Porky nodded his sack-covered head and suggested, ''Why don't you and Deputy Clancy just go back inside, Sheriff? Me and the boys will be proud to take over from here!''

The sheriff started to say something. Then, as if he'd grown weary of staring down the barrels of that Greener, he shrugged and turned away, motioning Deputy Clancy to fall in step with him once he'd made it that far alive.

As the two lawmen walked away from the tense confrontation by the stable door, Dancing Dave tried to live up to his name with some sudden footwork. But he was pistol-whipped and fell to his hands and knees in the moonlit dust, and other rough hands had laid hold of the sobbing Bubblehead, who didn't resist but got pistol-whipped in any case as he bawled he didn't like the way they were playing with him.

Both prisoners were bound with their wrists behind them and marched through the stable and out to where others waited with saddle broncs and a buckboard drawn by two mules.

''You boys are making a big mistake!'' yelled Dancing Dave as he and the weeping half-wit were thrown face-down across the wagonbed. But nobody seemed to be listening to either of them as the one called Porky called, ''Move it on out, boys!''

As the buckboard carried them to a fate only the train robber with a federal warrant on him seemed to grasp, Bubblehead Burnside sobbed, ''Why are they acting so mean to us, mister? I ain't been bad. Have you been bad?''

Dancing Dave Loman had been bad indeed, for some time. But some inner spark of warmth welled up from deep inside him as he said soothingly, ''Don't cry, old son. Crying ain't gonna help and it'll only make the bastards feel better about doing us dirty.''

Bubblehead sniffed, ''Why do they want to do us dirty, mister?''

To which the homicidal train robber beside him could only reply with a graveyard smile, ''Reckon they're just ornery. All I ever did was done for money. Hardly seems fair I'm about to die over an infernal Sunday school teacher I never laid eyes on! Was she pretty, this here Miss Mildred you admired so much?''

Bubblehead Burnside seemed to forget where they were, or the position he was in, as he smiled broadly and replied, ''Oh, Miss Mildred was real pretty, and real nice too. She told the other boys and girls not to laugh at me and call me names when I went over the lines.''

''Went over the *what*?''

''Coloring book lines,'' Bubblehead explained. ''Miss Mildred gave us crayons to color with and books with pictures of Baby Jesus and his mom. She said we could color them any way we liked as long as we didn't go over the lines. I *tried* not to go over the lines, but some of the time it was real hard not to, see?''

''You didn't have any notion what you were doing to her, did you?'' said Dancing Dave Loman. Then, before his fellow victim could reply, the buckboard under them suddenly stopped so that rough hands could drag them across the rough planking and drop them to the dust with rib-cracking thuds.

Then they were yanked back to their feet and marched out along the cross-ties of a railroad trestle spanning a deep dry draw. Only Dancing Dave grasped the full meaning of the hemp noose someone dropped over his head and drew tighter around his neck. Bubblehead had more trouble balancing on the less certain footing as the compact party proceeded almost joyfully out to the middle of the trestle. Everyone but

Dancing Dave laughed when Bubblehead asked if they were almost there yet.

The one called Porky declared in a jovial tone, "This ought to do well enough, boys." So they stopped. Two different members of the gang hunkered down to knot the other ends of the ropes around exposed railroad ties. Bubblehead asked if he could have a drink of water.

Porky pushed him off the trestle. Bubblehead's short but chunky body snapped the rope taut with a jolt that twanged the trestle under everyone's feet. Then, in the moment of silence that followed the loud snap, Dancing Dave Loman muttered, "You cold-hearted son of a bitch! You didn't even give the kid a chance to say his last—"

And then Dancing Dave Loman was flailing his longer legs through thin air as he too went off the trestle to drop down, and down some more, until the trestle twanged under everyone else.

Then Porky chuckled knowingly and declared for the edification of anyone who cared, "Hell, I *knew* what both them bastards wanted to say at the last. They wanted to say they were innocent. That's about all any of 'em ever have to say."

As he led the way back to solid ground and their waiting horseflesh, one of his followers thoughtfully opined, "That outlaw from other parts *was* innocent, as far as the crimes against Miss Mildred went. Ain't we likely to have trouble with Uncle Sam when that U.S. deputy marshal arrives to discover we've strung up a stranger with a federal warrant on him?"

Porky shrugged his massive shoulders. "What can he do to us, seeing ain't nobody in this county is about to tell him who done it? He's welcome to fume and fuss a mite before he gets back aboard the train to let us handle things our own way in these parts."

Someone else in the bunch asked, "What if he ain't content to fume and fuss? I heard over to the Red Rooster earlier they were sending that tall drink of water they calls Longarm.

He was up this way a spell back after some other old boys. I understand he just kept scouting for their sign until he *caught* 'em too!''

An even more worried voice cut in with: "I heard the same. That's how come they call him Longarm. What are we supposed to say if Longarm cuts our sign, Porky?''

Porky didn't answer as he shifted his ten-gauge Greener to remount his pony. There were some questions that were just too dumb to answer.

Chapter 2

The bodies hung side by side, long and short, all through the night. So they were both stiff as planks when they were hauled in to town the next morning. Doc Forbes, the part-time county coroner, allowed their rigor mortis would wear off by the time he could hold his official inquest. So they were left in his root cellar atop good stout planks that spanned the sawhorses. Doc Forbes hadn't kept potatoes and turnips down there since they'd elected him the coroner.

So that was where they lay, and how things stood, when the morning combination came up from Ogallala to deliver a tall rangy figure wearing a tobacco tweed suit between his dark pancaked Stetson and low-heeled cavalry stovepipes. He hadn't thought there was any call to haul along his old army saddle or Winchester '73. So he'd left them in his furnished digs on the unfashionable side of Denver's Cherry Creek. But he had leg irons in his one overnight bag to go with the handcuffs clipped to the back of his gun rig under his frock coat in case Dancing Dave Loman acted as frisky as some said he might. The same gun rig braced a double-action Colt .44-40 in its cross-draw holster on his left hip, with a double derringer clipped to one end of the watch chain across his tweed vest, should push come to shove.

The rail stop at Pawnee Junction had a handsome water tower and more than an acre of stockyards alongside the tracks. But passengers made do with an open sun-silvered platform, and settled up with the train crews getting on or getting off. A man getting off with only one bag didn't need any help. The sheriff and his three deputies were only there to howdy and explain.

Since the four local lawmen had their badges pinned to their vests, with the older gent's gold-plated, it was easy enough for a stranger to stick out his free hand and declare, "Morning, Sheriff Wigan. I'd be Deputy U.S. Marshal Custis Long of the Denver District Court, and I understand you picked up Dancing Dave Loman for us as he was enjoying a horizontal polka with one of your soiled doves?"

The older, taller sheriff shook hands with a sad little smile and replied, "We surely did, ah, Longarm. But I fear your long train ride from Denver has been in vain. Dancing Dave is dead. You're welcome to attend the inquest, of course. But if you do, you'll miss the last train headed south this evening."

Longarm whistled thoughtfully and asked, "What happened? Did he try to bust out on you?"

To which the sheriff could only reply with a sheepish expression, "He was busted out and lynched, along with a murdering rapist, along about last midnight. We doubt they were after your federal prisoner. But you know how such gents get, once they've passed the jug and worked themselves up to enjoy a hanging."

Longarm curled a lip under his heroic mustache and growled, "I do. I reckon my boss, Marshal Billy Vail, will be content with me arresting a handy half-dozen of the ringleaders. I'd be obliged for such help as you and your boys could give me, of course, and I'll be proud to put it in writing if it'll be of any use to you in the elections this fall."

Sheriff Wigan shot a warning glance at an incredulous-

10

looking kid deputy, swallowed, and said, "We'd sure be willing to help you if we could, Longarm. But nobody knows who the Minute Men might be!"

Longarm squinted up at the morning sun. "I just observed it was an election year. Seeing you can't point out any of your local registered voters, where might a stranger find a hotel in this fair haven of law and order?"

Before the sheriff could reply, one of his deputies suggested the Widow MacUlric's boardinghouse across from the municipal corral a furlong up the tracks.

Sheriff Wigan cut in. "Hold on. I was about to say you were welcome as rain if you'd like to stay at my place, Longarm!"

The younger but doubtless more experienced lawman smiled thinly and replied, not unkindly, "Thanks just the same. But if it's all the same with you, I'd as soon leave this bag in a regular boardinghouse. I got some valuable spare socks and a brand new bar of soap to worry about."

He started walking. Sheriff Wigan perforce tagged along, telling his deputies he'd see them all later at the office. As the two taller lawmen dropped off the end of the plank platform to trudge on along the crunchy railroad ballast between the tracks and weed-grown ditch, Wigan muttered, "They told me you could act hard-ass when the other kids wouldn't play mumbly-peg by your rules. But . . ."

"This ain't a kid's game," Longarm told him. "I said I followed your drift. I know I'm just a sometime annoyance that nobody in these parts will get to vote on, whether they're still pissed or not, come November. I know this is going to come as a swamping surprise to you, Sheriff, but I've investigated necktie parties in other parts in the past and, so far, I've yet to find a single county where everybody from the county prosecutor down to the saloon swampers didn't know most every member of the mob by name!"

Wigan insisted, "Things ain't that simple in these parts. To begin with, this sand hill range ain't been settled long enough for everyone to know everyone else by name. After that, our folks are divided some as to how you settle sand hill range. The cattlemen who were up this way first don't think too highly of the sodbusting homesteaders crowding in on us of late. So it ain't as if we wouldn't get us some unsigned mail if all that many knew just who the Minute Men *were*!''

Longarm grimaced and insisted, ''You've heard or read more than one name by now.'' His declarative statement left no leeway at all.

Wigan gulped again and said, ''Well, sure, we've had some fingers pointed. But like you just said, folks who go around accusing other folks ain't all that reliable. Even when they ain't lying, they seldom give you evidence you could use in court. Saying you heard somebody say they heard somebody brag they rode with the Minute Men don't cut no ice with any jury because no judge worth spit would ever allow you to *present* such evidence in his court in the first place!''

Longarm said, ''I've noticed that. How far is that boardinghouse and how come you keep calling your neighborhood lynch mobs Minute Men?''

The sheriff pointed off to their right at some dusty stock lazing in a big pole corral. ''That mustard-colored two-story frame house near the red livery on the far side. They call the bunch who lynched your prisoner the Minute Men because that's the way they act. Ready to ride at a minute's notice, see?''

''No, I don't,'' said Longarm flatly. ''The Minute Men who fought and died at Lexington and Concord were no part of any *mob*! They were lawfully assembled colonial militiamen, enlisted under their true names without one fool mask between them. Rightly or wrongly, they stood their ground under officers commissioned by their elected New England assemblies. They were only called Minute Men when they were on detached active service, ordered to stay ready to

12

report back to their posts at a minute's notice. Are you saying the sons of bitches who lynched my prisoner last night were members of the Nebraska National Guard?''

Wigan smiled uncertainly and replied, ''Don't get you bowels in an uproar at *me*! I never named our own Minute Men the Minute Men. I only said they *called* their fool selves the Minute Men!''

Longarm replied in a more mollified tone, ''Fool selves is the term I was groping for. Like old Abe Lincoln said, you can *call* the tail of a dog its fifth leg all you want. But the dog's still going to wag its tail and walk around on its four legs. You say these insults to the *real* Minute Men murdered another prisoner last night along with Dancing Dave Loman?''

As they circled the dusty corral Sheriff Wigan related the sad tale of Bubblehead Burnside, a hitherto harmless village idiot gone wrong. Longarm agreed he'd heard similar sad tales in other parts, sometimes with similar results. He made a wry face and added, ''I don't sec why some old boys can't wait for a public hanging everyone in town could enjoy. From what you say, that Burnside kid never stood a chance of beating murder in the first with premeditated rape thrown in.''

Wigan sighed and said, ''That's on account you never laid eyes on Bubblehead Burnside, no offense. He was over twenty-one, but the county court had declared him incompetent to fend for himself and made him a ward of his normal older sister, Miss Rose Burnside. When we came to her place on the edge of town to arrest him, after he'd raped and stabbed Miss Mildred, we found him out back on his hands and knees, playing marbles in the dirt with the chickens.''

Longarm shrugged and said, ''My boss, Billy Vail, wouldn't have cared. What a feeble-minder did to anybody up this way wouldn't have been a matter for the Denver District Court. But now that the same lynch mob that came for Burnside murdered a federal prisoner in the bargain, I

13

reckon I'd best look into your whole damn bucket of spit. What time might they be holding that coroner's inquest, and where?''

Wigan said, ''Doc Forbes is planning to autopsy the two of 'em this afternoon, with some expert from the Pawnee Agency helping. Says he'll present his findings to the panel in the back room of our courthouse about seven. It seems a tad late in the day, I know. But Miss Rose has been a tidy neighbor, save for her spooky kid brother, and she's anxious to have the little shit embalmed and boxed in his Sunday-go-to-meeting duds. From the way she's been carrying on, you'd think she was still fond of him, despite all he's done to shame her.''

Longarm didn't ask where the county courthouse might be. As they crossed the dusty street between the municipal corral and lined-up frame buildings beyond, Longarm told the sheriff he'd see him later at the inquest. Wigan looked confounded and declared, ''It's early yet. You sure you can't use some guidance and introductions betwixt now and late this evening?''

Longarm shook his head and replied, not unkindly but firmly, that he liked to work alone. He felt no call to add he'd found he got more out of folks when their local law wasn't listening in.

So they shook on it and parted friendly. Then Longarm opened the gate of the low picket fence in front of that mustard-colored house to stride between knee-high dusty flowers, mount the recently swept front steps, and twist the polished brass turn-key of the boardinghouse doorbell.

A pale dusty blonde in a dusty tan smock opened the door for him with a turkey feather duster in one hand. It took a lot of dusting when you kept house across from a municipal corral. Longarm smiled down at the obvious parlor maid and introduced himself with a flash of his badge and identification before he asked if he might by any chance speak with the lady of the house.

14

The gal he'd taken for her hired help smiled wanly up at him and replied, "I'm the Widow MacUlric. My friends call me Mavis. If I didn't have more than enough rooms to let I wouldn't be doing my own housework. I can let you have a nice corner room overlooking the garden out back, along with three meals a day, for three dollars a week."

Longarm replied, "That sounds more than fair, Miss Mavis, but I don't know how long I'll be here, or how often I might or might not be coming in or out. So why don't you let me charge a dollar a day to my field expenses and might you have a *front* room I could hire, facing that corral across the way?"

She pointed at the nearby stairs with her duster as she told him uncertainly, "I'm in no position to turn down a dollar a day. So we can put you in the less comfortable front room I've been using myself, if you'll give me time to move some bedding and belongings. Why would anyone else care to bed down with the window facing into the south across that dusty corral all day?"

Then she blinked up at him. "Oh! You did say you were a lawman up here *after* somebody, and that *is* a *public* corral, isn't it?"

As he followed her up the stairs, admiring the view, even though her swaying hips seemed sort of skinny under that tan smock, Longarm soberly observed, "It surely is, ma'am. I understand they got this one street corner in London Town, near some place called Pick Your Dilly, where they say that if you wait there long enough, everyone in the world is sure to pass by sooner or later."

She gasped. "Good heavens, are you suggesting wanted outlaws have been riding in and out of the municipal corral, right under my front window, without my ever suspecting a thing?"

To which Longarm could only reply, "You've been running a boardinghouse. You ain't paid to keep an eye peeled for outlaws. I carry a gun and a badge. So they expect me to suspect things, ma'am."

Chapter 3

Longarm offered to help. But the Widow MacUlric insisted housework was women's work. So he allowed he'd be back for noon dinner, and strode over to the Western Union near the railroad stop.

Once there, he wired his home office the little he'd found out so far. He didn't ask Marshal Billy Vail whether he was supposed to arrest anybody or not. Western Union charged a nickel a word for flat-rate wires and old Billy could be such a fuss about needless waste when he went over a deputy's field expenses.

Longarm stopped by a tobacco shop for some three-for-a-nickel cheroots and the latest gossip on last night's lynchings. He wound up with two bits worth of smokes and as much information as he might have gotten from the wooden Indian standing out front.

It was early in the day for any responsible citizens to be sipping suds in the one saloon that was open at that hour. So Longarm tried the barbershop he spied across the way. He didn't need a haircut, but a man could always use a store-bought shave this late in the day if he needed an excuse to wait his turn and jaw a mite.

There were four morning customers ahead of him. Three townies and what seemed like a prosperous cowhand indeed. The rascal must have weighed three hundred pounds. He was only saved from looking just plain sissy-fat by standing well over six feet, and that was before he put on those high-heeled Justins he wore with his sailcloth pants legs tucked inside. His black sateen shirt and maroon brocaded vest had likely set him back more than his black Texas hat. But not as much as the brace of silver-mounted and ivory-handled Remington .45s riding his broad hips in tooled black leather holsters.

Longarm could see all this at a glance because the big beefy cuss rose when Longarm entered, as if he'd been expected.

But when Longarm nodded at the big rider, the big rider never said anything as he barely nodded back. Longarm could see the one barber wasn't nearly finished with his current customer. So he figured the stockman had just grown tired of sitting in the bentwood chair he'd risen from. There were plenty of seats that morning. So Longarm felt no call to thank anyone for offering him one as he sat down near the doorway. There was a folded newspaper on the empty chair next to the one he'd chosen. He picked it up and scanned the front page a spell before he declared to nobody in particular, ''I see they ain't printed anything about that necktie party we had last night yet.''

Nobody said a word or even glanced his way. Small-town barbershops could be that way. He went on. ''The reason I mentioned current events is that I am Deputy U.S. Marshal Custis Long of the Denver District Court and I was sent all this way to gather up the one they called Dancing Dave and deliver him to another hangman entirely. I find it more peculiar than annoying that somebody up this way hung Dancing Dave at less expense to the federal district I ride for. Dancing Dave Loman had done wonders and eaten cucumbers in other parts of this great land. But it was my under-

17

standing he was hiding out in Nebraska because this was about the only state he wasn't wanted in.''

The balding barber shot him a stern look by way of the big wall mirror and demanded, "Did you come in here for a shave, a haircut, or to gossip like an old fishwife?"

Before Longarm could answer, the bulky stockman standing near the back wall with a gun on each hip laughed jovially and cut in to take the bit in his own teeth, declaring, "Lawman has a right to be nosy when the Minute Men string up a cuss he'd had his heart set on.''

Beaming down at Longarm, who was fighting the temptation to rise and adjust his own gun rig, the just as tall and far wider two-gun man explained, "That's last week's edition of the *Monitor,* pilgrim. They ain't had time to report what happened in these parts last night. I ain't saying I was there myself, you understand, but I reckon I can tell you why they robbed you of your own true love. That train robber had the misfortune of being locked up with the murderous son of a bitch the Minute Men were *really* after. They were after Bubblehead Burnside because he raped and murdered a pretty church lady, and because they knew the son-of-a-bitching circuit judge was likely to send the knave to that insane asylum over to Omaha!''

There came a rumble of agreement—now that the bully had told them what their opinions had better well be. A townsman in a snuff-colored outfit opined, "They should have locked that loony away years ago. Always knew Bubblehead Burnside was going to hurt somebody someday. Had half the kids in town scared skinny, coming at them all squinty-eyed and drooling as he asked 'em to shoot marbles with him!''

Another customer volunteered, "And him a grown man of nearly four and twenty too! I mind what you just said about him and the little kids. Had poor Mildred Powell heeded the *other* ladies, she might be alive today! Nobody else but poor Miss Mildred wanted the idiot attending her Sunday school

18

classes. They told her it wasn't natural or healthy to have a full-grown man drooling at her over coloring books that way."

The bigger man standing by the back wall stared thoughtfully down at Longarm as he declared, "Our Denver lawman ain't interested in the droolings of Bubblehead Burnside. He's more concerned with the rope dance of Dancing Dave Lowman. Ain't that right, Longarm?"

There was common courtesy, and there was common sense when a man with two guns in quick-draw holsters was smiling down at you that way. So Longarm rose to his own considerable height, his frock coat open to expose the more modest grips of his own .44-40 as he calmly replied, "It surely is, and might you have a name of your own, old son, seeing you seem to know *me* so well?"

"I'd be Porky Shaw, boss wrangler out to the Diamond B," the big man answered easily. He added, "Knew who you were as soon as you opened your mouth because you're more famous. We'd heard you were headed up this way to carry that train robber back to Denver."

"Is that why you hung him?" Longarm asked as easily.

It got very quiet for the next million years. Then Porky Shaw laughed incredulously and demanded, "Are you accusing me or anyone else here of stringing them boys up last night?"

Longarm smiled thinly and replied, "I ain't as worried about *who* as *why*. You were right about us having our hearts set on a serious conversation with Dancing Dave. Aside from his own misdeeds, he was in a swell position to clear up some other matters for us. Any man given his choice of talking about his gang or dancing at the end of a rope is likely to choose talking."

Porky Shaw looked sincerely puzzled as he asked, "Didn't you just now say the cuss hadn't done anything to anyone up our way?"

Longarm nodded soberly and replied, "That's why I find

his death so mysterious. *We* wanted him alive, to talk to us. More than one of his former business associates would have paid good money to see him dead so's he couldn't. I'll be switched with snakes if I can fathom why a purely local mob of cowardly assholes would want to lynch old Dancing Dave. Unless, of course, they like to jack off in unison to the thrill of watching somebody die.''

The barber froze in mid-snip. Nobody else in the confined space seemed to be breathing as Porky Shaw's fat face changed colors back and forth between ash and beet while he chose his words with some care. Then, as Longarm calmly studied him as if he'd been a bug on a pin, Porky blustered, ''Them's mighty hard words for men you don't know, Denver boy.''

Longarm quietly but firmly answered, ''I know them. If not by name, I know them by their cur-dog snarly laughter as they egg one another on to cowardly heroics. Dancing Dave had his faults, and from what you say that marble-shooting sex maniac couldn't have been a man I'd care to drink with. But ain't it curious how not a single one of your so called Minute Men had the grit to face either of 'em man to man?''

As Porky Shaw's fat face went from frog belly back to smoked ham, the barber interjected soothingly, ''Come on. Be fair, Longarm! It ain't as if our Minute Men had no just cause! Suppose *you* found a pretty young church lady all cut up and dying. Then suppose she flat out told you she'd been ravaged and stabbed by a drooling idiot she'd tried to be nice to! What would you do if you'd known the poor gal personal and you knew the law was likely to let her killer live?''

Longarm shrugged and said, ''I'd kill him. I wouldn't go home to get my mask and wait around until me and all my pals could screw up the nerve to come slithering like snakes after sundown.''

Porky Shaw blustered, ''The Minute Men ain't sneaks! They ain't any mob! They're a sort of secret posse or militia organized to keep law and order in these parts, see?''

Longarm laughed coldly and glanced thoughtfully at the Regulator Brand clock above the mirror as he said, ''I didn't know the saloons had been open that long this morning. I hope you won't take this as mean-spirited, Porky, but a mob is still a mob no matter what anybody wants to call it. Secret posse is a contradiction in terms. Under the rules of common law, going back before Robin Hood and that mean Sheriff of Nottingham, a posse comitatus is a temporary but lawfully assembled gathering of the able-bodied men of a county, sworn in under the sheriff of the county, to follow said sheriff's orders.''

He let that sink in before he continued. ''Whether he was in the wrong or in the right, old Robin Hood had no powers under common law to swear his merry men of the forest in as a posse comitatus. Like the book says, Robin and his merry men were *outlaws,* no matter how fair or unfair they thought the laws were at the time.''

Porky Shaw grumbled, ''Hell, don't fuss at me about the way them Minute Men are organized. *I* never organized them!''

Longarm said, ''*Somebody* must have, and I'd sure like to tell him what an asshole he was if he even hinted they were *militia.* For I've heard tell you have men in these parts who rode for both sides in the war, and calling another bunch a *militia* could be taken as an insult to the memories of many a real militiaman in blue or gray!''

A younger townie who'd been trying not to say anything burst out with, ''Hold on, I knew the Ohio Volunteers were militia, but what was that about them Johnny Rebs?''

''Militia. Lawfully enlisted by the elected state assemblies of both sides,'' Longarm replied with a nod. ''That's how come we call state troops the National Guard now. From way before the American Revolution up to the elections of 1860, the governor of each colony and then state was empowered to recruit and organize a militia, or body of part-time troops, to call out in times of trouble against, say, raiding French and Indians or pesky redcoats. The point to bear in mind is that such militia units were open and aboveboard organizations approved by their local government, with nobody wearing masks or enlisted under phony names.''

The barber snorted, ''Hell, if our Minute Men gave out their right names, they'd never be able to uphold law and order around here without winding up in state prison!''

To which Longarm replied with a sardonic smile, ''I just said that. Real militiamen carry out the orders of their lawfully constituted governments period, with no ifs, ands, or buts. I wasn't there, but I've read the reports handed in by Captain Parker of the *real* Minute Men and Major Pitcairn of the Royal Marines, after the gunfight at Lexington Green. Nobody on either side was saying he was somebody else. Captain Parker allowed he was acting in his lawful capacity as a commissioned officer of the Massachusetts Assembly when he demanded to know where all those redcoats were headed without any search warrant. And we know what happened after that. The first shots of the more recent war were fired by honest soldiers with *their* bare faces hanging out too! As the Southern states left the Union, or tried to, they called up their lawful state militias, just as the Northern states called their own already organized outfits to active duty. The end result was a Union Army whupping a Confederate Army, with the victors stripping all state governments of the powers to carry things that far in the future by federalizing all state militias. But we were talking about what is and what's *not* a posse comitatus or a militia, and anyone can see the rascals who lynched a federal prisoner last night were neither one nor the other!''

''The hell you say!'' snapped Porky Shaw, bracing his boot heels wider as he continued in an ominous tone. ''It just so happens some kith and kin of mine rode with William Clarke Quantrill's Fifth Confederate Cav, and I don't recall anything about *them* starting out as any state militia outfit.''

22

Longarm nodded agreeably and replied, "Nobody but Quantrill ever implied they might have been. Neither Quantrill, Bloody Bill Anderson, Frank James, nor Cole Younger were ever enlisted in any real military unit, North or South. They were a piss-ant bunch of pure-ass bandits raiding along the Missouri-Kansas border on their own without as much as a note to the teacher from any elected official of the Confederacy."

"Are you calling my very own kith and kin a bunch of liars?" the hulking boss wrangler choked out.

Longarm moved clear of his vacated seat as he quietly pointed out, "You were the one who said they rode with Quantrill and his pure outlaw regiment. But should you feel insulted I'm at your service, Pork Pie."

Porky Shaw looked as if he was either going to slap leather or piss his pants. But then he spoiled all the fun by licking his pale lips and blustering, "We'd best cut out this kid stuff before somebody calls the law on us. I ain't afraid of you personal, Longarm. But we both know what a time I'd have explaining once I beat you to the draw."

"Don't you mean *if* you beat me to the draw?" asked Longarm mildly.

"Don't the rest of you see what he's trying to do here?" the big boss wrangler asked the barber in an almost pleading voice.

The barber sighed and said, "Sure. It was your own grand notion to start up with him, Porky. I never talk to strangers if I don't have to. That's how come I'm so much older than you're ever likely to wind up at the rate you're going."

Porky choked back some words that might have been meant for anyone in the shop. Then he circled around the far side of the barber's chair, blustered out the corner door, and stomped off down the walk.

The barber made a wry face at Longarm and declared, "If I was you I'd be on my own way as well. He's liable to be coming back with some friends, and I don't reckon you know who you were just talking to!''

Longarm moved over to stand with his own back to the wall as he quietly replied, ''Golly, I sure hope you're right. I *know* who I must have been talking to. I just don't know how I'd be able to *prove* it unless I can encourage him to stop acting so friendly.''

Chapter 4

The World Atlas allowed that the Sand Hill Country of western Nebraska enjoyed, or suffered, a "continental climate." That meant cold as a banker's heart in the winter and hot as a whore's pillow on payday in the summer. So Longarm was sweating under his shoestring tie and tweed frock coat by the time he made it back to the Widow MacUlric's for that noon dinner she'd promised.

She met him in the hall to say she was serving out back under her grape arbor, and he almost kissed her when she added the gents would be served in their shirtsleeves without ties, seeing it was getting hot enough to hard-boil eggs under the hen.

Longarm went upstairs to the front room he'd hired in order to hang up his hat and coat. He gained more respect for their thoughtful young landlady when he felt how hot the room she usually bunked in could get facing south at noon. The fresh linens on the modest iron-pipe bedstead were clean but threadbare, and there were other signs of barely getting by in evidence. There were no rugs on the oiled plank flooring, and while three walls had been papered cheaply to display cheerful orange blossoms unknown to botany against a spinach-green and mustard-yellow background, they'd run out of regular wallpaper and made do along one side wall with what seemed to be Confederate war bonds and defunct stock certificates. The smaller rectangles of engraved bond paper were neatly applied so that all the dignified old gents and newfangled steam engines that had likely never been built were right side up.

Longarm left his vest buttoned, but got rid of that fool tie he'd been expected to wear on duty since President Hayes and Miss Lemonade Lucy had moved into the White House. He considered hanging up his gun rig. He'd still have his vest-pocket derringer if anybody fought him for second helpings. But he remembered that barber's warning, and more than one old boy had been shot over a picket fence as he was dining al fresco out back. So he went back downstairs with his .44-40 riding cross-draw and suddenly feeling more awkward against his hip.

But nobody else seemed to notice when he joined the party of four other boarders and Miss Mavis under the grape arbor out back. Everyone but the landlady was seated at a trestle table, with mismatched china spread on worn but spotless linen. As he was introduced to the three gents and one young gal, it developed that all four were single working folk without any kin in these parts. So Longarm felt free to pay more attention to the small brunette library gal than the two clerks and a skinny gent who said he stuck type for the *Pawnee Junction Advertiser*. Miss Ellen Brent, the librarian, was cute as a button, and once he knew the *Advertiser* was the Republican paper in these parts, he figured nobody working for it would know more than *he* did about the so-called Minute Men.

There were almost always at least two local papers, partial to the two factions you almost always had in your average county. The business folks and smallholders tended to vote Republican in Nebraska. Cattle barons, and the hands who worked for them, tended to vote Grange or Democrat out this way. Porky Shaw had bragged on being the boss wrangler of the Diamond B, and a cow spread had to grow a bit before you got to brag on its brand.

Longarm knew, from earlier scouting in the Sand Hill Country, how many a Union vet had headed west to homestead out Nebraska way while many an unreconstructed Texican Reb had been driving his longhorns up to the greener north ranges to replace the buffalo and horse Indian. Adventure writers such as old Ned Buntline tended to make a big whoop-de-doo over cowboys and Indians down in the cactus country along the Rio Grande or Gila, but if anybody wanted to worry about gunsmoke on the wild frontier, the *tense* frontier ran just west of longitude 100°, from the chaparral of Chihuahua to the Peace River Range of Canada, where the long grass met the short grass and a man could argue either way about plowing or grazing it.

Neither murder-rapes nor midnight lynchings made for proper mealtime talk, even if he'd thought anyone there knew anything about what seemed like a bunch of surly range riders. So Longarm just ate and allowed the others to do most of the talking. None of it was all that interesting. It was easy but hardly unusual to compliment the Widow MacUlric on her plain but hearty fare. Once you'd allowed she salted stew just right and mashed spuds smooth, there was no need to lie about her sort of weak coffee. The poor gal was doing her best to get by. Four boarders at three bucks apiece gave her twelve a week to run this place on. So she had some other financial woes that didn't show. Likely a mortgage. It wouldn't have been polite to ask, and Billy Vail hadn't sent him up this way to study Pawnee Junction real estate in any case.

She'd made a too-sweet apple pie with lots of corn starch for dessert. There was no cheese to go with the apple pie. He idly wondered if she might be a solitary drinker. Such folks tended to have a sweet tooth as well as financial problems. But she didn't look like she was up to anything unhealthy when she wasn't wading through housework up to her hips. Having debts to pay off made more sense. It was easy as hell for a widow woman to wind up in debt.

Miss Ellen from the library helped the widow clear the table as the gents leaned back to light up. Longarm decided the little library gal wasn't as stuck on herself as she had every right to be since the taller and thinner widow woman said right out she could manage by herself and didn't expect her boarders to pitch in. But when Miss Ellen stamped with her high-button shoe and went right on rolling up the sleeves of her seersucker bodice, Miss Mavis smiled at her fondly as hell and the two of them made short work of that table.

As soon as he figured it wouldn't be rude, Longarm took leave of his fellow boarders, went back up to get his hat, and got back to work in his shirtsleeves by one in the afternoon.

He found his way to the county coroner's frame house in a nicer part of town, and got there just as the neighborly Doc Forbes, a portly gray figure, was helping his own old woman clear *their* dinner table.

Forbes allowed he'd heard Longarm was in town and that he'd been expecting him. Forbes said, ''I haven't more than had them stripped and hosed down as yet. I sent for a young B.I.A. practical nurse at the Pawnee Agency. She may be lacking a degree, but I've read her paper the *New England Journal of Medicine* saw fit to publish and I fear she may know more than me about the condition the Burnside boy was suffering from. Nurse Nancy Calder sent in a mighty detailed study of those feeble-minded Pawnee kids she's been trying to help. It's not good medical practice to lump all such unfortunates together, and Nurse Calder didn't. Two out of the five Indian kids she studied read as if they could be long-lost kin to the pure-white Bubblehead Burnside. His real name was Howard, but Bubblehead fit so much better.''

As Doc Forbes led him inside, Longarm idly asked what difference it made once a feeble-minded unfortunate had acted really dumb and been murdered by a mob.

28

Forbes said, "Easier to show you than to argue about it. Come on, I have them both set up for autopsy down below."

Longarm followed the older man along the shady corridor and down a gloomy flight of stairs to a musty but cooler cellar. Doc Forbes lit a candle at the foot of the steps and pointed at a heavy wooden door down at one end. Longarm followed him to an even lower, cooler, and worse-smelling root cellar. Forbes raised the candle to light an oil lamp hanging just above their heads between two ominous-looking sheet-draped forms reclining at waist height.

Shaking out the match and tossing it to the dirt floor, Doc Forbes removed the sheet from the longer cadaver as he declared, "This would be the remains of your train-robbing David Lowman, a Union veteran who should have quit while he was ahead. I make it fourteen old wounds all told. That bullet scar on his right thigh being no more than three years old."

Longarm stared soberly down at the cadaver grinning up at him so cheerfully and replied, "That's Dancing Dave, all right. He got shot in the leg by a Pinkerton man three years ago, like you said. But there's nothing on his yellow sheets about his war record."

Doc Forbes pointed casually at an ugly triangular scar near the hip of that same shot-up leg, waiting for Longarm to say something.

Longarm nodded and said, "Sure. That's an old bayonet wound. Some units on both sides were issued those same trifoil French bayonets. Nasty sons of bitches to get stuck with, but neither Union nor Confederate in particular."

Forbes nodded, then pointed at the dead man's bare left shoulder.

Longarm brightened and said, "I should have looked for that right off. I caught an old Texas rider in a lie one time when he let me see the Union Army vaccination mark he shouldn't have received had he *really* ridden with Hood's Texas Brigade."

Doc Forbes nodded and volunteered, "No pinpoints of blood in the whites of his eyes. So he died instantly when he hit the end of the rope. You can see without cutting into him how the snap completely separated his neck vertebrae. We'll open him later to make sure he wasn't fed prussic acid. But he's not the mystery."

Forbes whipped another sheet from the remains of Bubblehead Burnside and said, "Here lies the mystery."

Longarm stared down at the shorter, stockier body with more distaste than interest. It was easy to see why they'd called the dead youth Bubblehead. He'd been an unfortunate type Longarm had seen more than once in the past. Still gripped in rigor mortis, the moon-faced and squint-eyed kid of fair complexion was grinning wider than he'd likely grinned in life. It was hard to believe even a village idiot could go about looking that idiotic for long.

Doc Forbes said, "Never mind his face. What do you have to say about the rest of him?"

Longarm swept his gaze down the naked nearly hairless cadaver to note the short chunky arms and sort of bearlike torso. Then he saw the dead boy's privates had been nothing to brag about either. They said it was cruel to speak ill of the dead, but fair was fair and so Longarm had to opine, "I've seen twelve-year-old boys hung better. No pubic hair at all around that little bitty pud, and you say he *raped* that church lady before he stuck a knife in her?"

Doc Forbes said, "No. *She* did, with her last dying breath. She might have been confused. I naturally examined *her* body for the county before we released it to her family for the funeral. It's not as easy to determine virginity as some think, but if this poor defective *did* get inside her with the little he had to offer, he failed to ejaculate. That's easy to determine."

Longarm wrinkled his nose as he stared down at the child-like sex organs of the dead half-wit. He said, "Well, sometimes there's more than first meets the eye when a man rises fully to the occasion. So let's say he got it in, or *tried* to get it in, enough to really upset your average Sunday school teacher. Then suppose she laughed at him, or he *thought* she was laughing at him, when he just wasn't the man to rape her right.''

Doc Forbes shrugged and said, ''As a country doctor I can tell you many a man with all his wits about him can get mighty upset when his old organ-grinder fails him at the last minute. So who's to say what sort of a rage an idiot such as this might fly into when he couldn't get his warped flesh to obey his perverse lust?''

''I can tell you,'' declared a firm feminine voice from the darkness near the doorway as both surprised men swung their gaze her way.

Nurse Nancy Calder stepped into the circle of light dressed more for riding than for tending sick Indians. Her brown hair was bound up under a straw boater and her tan poplin riding habit was stained with sweat, dust, or both, depending on which part of her junoesque curves one admired. Longarm felt awkward about the two naked dead men in her presence, but from the way both Doc Forbes and his visitor acted, they both seemed to take such sights in stride.

After a dismissive glance at the dead outlaw, Nurse Calder looked more thoughtfully at the remains of Bubblehead Burnside, nodded as if she knew, and flatly stated, ''Mongolism. An almost classic example. It's harder to be certain with Indians because some of them can have the backs of their heads flattened by cradle boards without really suffering the condition. You never see a fair-featured white child with those eyes and that skull shape without the other features of the syndrome, though.''

Moving around to the far side of the dead half-wit, she took one stiff wrist in hand and raised the plump palm to the lamplight as she pontificated, ''Look at these abnormal palm lines and the way the last finger curves inward. There's a one-in-four chance he suffered a heart defect as well. But I see somebody broke his poor neck for him before he could die young as most of them do!''

''He was lynched, ma'am,'' Longarm told her, asking, ''You say folks like him are *Mongolians*?''

Nurse Calder shook her straw boater firmly and replied, ''No. They look that way no matter what their ancestry might be. Children with this birth defect are born to women of all races in about the same numbers. A rough average of one out of five hundred deliveries. The statistics were compiled and the symptoms were first described in a scientific manner back in '66 by a Dr. Langdon Down. He described them as *Mongoloid* because of superficial racial resemblance. He showed how cruel the snide remarks about family trees and the sad Mongoloid idiots themselves proved to be. The few cases I've been privileged to examine all seemed to bear out Dr. Down's assertion that, in the main, Mongoloid idiots tend to have placid, friendly dispositions. Most are fond of music and simple games. They seldom if ever commit any crimes, few of them seem to know how to lie, and they almost never lose their tempers, even when others tease them.''

Longarm stared down at the short but stocky accused killer as he declared, ''Once would be more than enough if the victim was caught by total surprise.''

Doc Forbes said, ''Seeing Nurse Calder's arrived, I'd as soon start the autopsies now. You might as well leave now, Deputy Long. We'll present all our findings at the hearing in writing, and from here on this is likely to seem unpleasant to a layperson.''

Longarm said, ''I ain't no layperson. I'm the law. So you all just slice away and I'll stick around, if it's all the same with you.''

Chapter 5

Like many a self-educated man, Longarm read more than he let on, and he took interest in almost anything scientific. But he was just as glad he'd never been pals with either of the dead men by the time the doc and Nurse Calder got through taking them apart. The gaping Y-shaped incisions from nipples to pubic bones were bad enough. The way they peeled the foreheads down to saw open the skulls could set a man's teeth on edge the way fingernails on a blackboard might.

The only interesting details they dug out of the late Dancing Dave were a couple of encysted bullets he'd been packing under his hide with no apparent ill effects. Nurse Calder seemed disappointed to discover Bubblehead Burnside's heart and lungs had been just about the same as a regular young gent's. She said Mongoloid idiots seldom made it to middle age. But that Bubblehead might have, had they *let* him. She was less surprised than Doc Forbes after they had both their brains bobbing in pickle jars of preservative. She said what she called the gross anatomy of most idiots' brains wasn't all that different to the naked eye. She said another doc named P. P. Broca, over in France, had been poking about in human brains enough to notice some *few* mental defects seemed to be caused by bumps and bruises you could see. But after that it was tough to tell how smart anyone had been, or even what race they'd been, just from looking at their brains.

She wanted to take the Mongoloid's brain home with her anyhow, to compare it with some Indian brains. Doc Forbes said she'd have to get permission from the next of kin, the dead boy having been white and hence entitled to less casual disposal than your average Indian.

Longarm figured he could excuse himself without looking girlish by the time they'd started sewing the first body back up with stout butcher's twine. So he went upstairs to see if lighting a cheroot out on the back porch might get his saliva to tasting better.

But when he got to the top of the stairs the doc's motherly old wife headed him off to allow they had a problem. He said he'd help if he could. So she led him through the kitchen and pointed out back through the lace curtains.

A one-horse hearse was parked in the alley by the doc's back gate. A couple of gents dressed in black, with crepe hanging down from the back brims of their stovepipe hats, lounged awkwardly just inside the open gate. A feminine figure in a veiled hat and rusty black dress was seated bolt upright on the front seat of the graveyard transport.

"Family?" asked Longarm quietly.

Mrs. Forbes said, "Rose Burnside, the only family the poor idiot had. She insisted on riding along to pick up the body. The boys from the undertaker's only brought the usual wicker hamper, and you must have just seen the present state of the remains."

Longarm nodded in understanding and said, "The problem is how they get old Bubblehead past her until they can make him a tad presentable. What if we could lure her into your front parlor long enough for the pick-up crew to nip in and out with their corpse hamper?"

The coroner's wife said, "I've already tried. She refused

34

my cake and coffee just now. The poor thing's dreadfully upset and hardly in the mood for socializing this afternoon.''

Longarm nodded thoughtfully. Then he brightened and said, "I ain't paid to socialize. I'm the law. So there may be another way to slice these onions.''

He opened the back door, strode boldly down the brick path to the hearse parked out back, barely nodding at its two man crew, and ticked the brim of his Stetson to the small dark figure perched up on its leather-padded seat, declaring in a no-nonsense tone, "I'd be Deputy U.S. Marshal Custis Long, and I'm sorry to intrude on your grief at a time like this, Miss Burnside. But I have some official questions to ask you, if you'd be good enough to come inside with me right now.''

It was hard to make out the veiled gal's expression, but she gasped in dismay before she asked if she was under arrest.

Longarm held out a hand to help her down as he replied in a firm tone, "That's for me to decide after we've had us a serious talk, Miss Rose.'' He shot a meaningful glance at the confused undertaking crew as he added in a more brotherly tone, "Some things are best discussed in private, ma'am.''

That did it. In no time at all Longarm had Rose Burnside seated on a horsehair sofa in the Forbes front parlor with Mrs. Forbes serving that cake and coffee in spite of all protests. Then she left the two of them alone, so they could talk in private and so she could signal the boys out back to get a move on as soon as her husband and Nurse Calder were ready for them.

With the cake and coffee in front of her on the rosewood coffee table between her sofa and Longarm's casual chair, Rose Burnside had to lift her veil up out of the way. As she draped it atop her black straw hat, Longarm saw a slight family resemblance in the complexion and hair coloring. Otherwise, she seemed just a blandly nice-looking woman of around thirty, give or take a lot of recent tears. Her eyes were red where they weren't blue, but they didn't slant worth mentioning. Her nose had more bridge to it than her kid brother's. As if she could read his mind, Rose Burnside said, "We had another brother who seemed normal too. He was killed fighting Comanche with the Texas Rangers years ago. You had to show common sense before the Rangers would enlist you, right?"

Longarm nodded soberly and said, "Neither the mental capacity of yourself or anyone else in your family is at issue, Miss Rose. I wish there was a kinder way to put it it, but ... You were told what your younger brother was accused of when they arrested him, right?"

She put her coffee cup back down untasted, but didn't blubber up on him as she replied in a dead certain tone, "Howard didn't do it. He loved Mildred Powell. I mean he loved her in a pure childlike way. He told me so himself."

She looked past him at a fern in the bay window as she added in a sort of peevish way, "He had this way of telling you the same thing, over and over, no matter how many times you told him that was enough. I'm sure I'd have known had he been hankering after any woman in the way they accused him of hankering after that Sunday school teacher."

"Somebody more than hankered for her," Longarm pointed out, gently adding, "You don't sound as if you thought too highly of the victim, no offense."

Rose Burnside grimaced and said, "If she led poor Howard on enough to drive him that wild, she might have had what happened to her coming! Have you any idea what it's like to be teased and teased all the time you were growing up?"

Longarm said, "I can imagine it some. We ain't talking about your *kid brother's* teasings, are we, Miss Rose?"

She started to cry some more. Longarm moved over beside her to put a comforting arm around her heaving shoulders as she sobbed, "Look at the Chinaman's big sister! Has your mother's Chinee got around to *you* yet, Rose, Rose, every-body knows?''

Longarm gently assured her, ''I have it on good authority that the condition ain't caused by Oriental ancestry, Miss Rose.''

She sobbed, ''Didn't you think I knew that? Didn't you think we *all* knew none of us had done anything to deserve Howard? My other brother left home for Texas at fourteen. Lord only knows where our poor mother ran off to after our father died. But I can understand how bearing the shame alone became just too much for her.''

Longarm shook his head, patted her shoulder, and quietly told her, ''No, you can't. You stayed on, and took care of him when there was nobody else. They told me you'd had the county declare him your ward, Miss Rose. You didn't have to. You could have wiggled out of it and left him to the mercy of the state. But you never did, and I can't hardly be the only one who thinks you did a proud thing. Like I said, I had to ask, and they had to tell me.''

She stopped shaking, but still looked mighty grim as she heaved a vast sigh and decided, ''What's done is done and it's almost over at last. Would it spoil the saintly image you have of me, ah, Custis, if I confessed I'm sort of *relieved* about not having to worry about poor Howard anymore?''

He smiled thinly and assured her, ''You're just being more honest than some saints, Miss Rose. Like everyone's said, you done proud by your unfortunate kid brother, and at least now you'll be free to get on with your life. I understand you have a homestead out to the edge of town?''

She shrugged and said, ''Forty acres, sixteen red duroc hogs, and a mule for sale. I'm selling my pony, Grassy. But I'm changing his name to something sensible as I sell out, mount up, and move on. Do I have to tell you who named a fourteen-hands paint Grassy or why?''

Longarm said, ''Well, he might have noticed the new pony liked to eat grass. I follow your drift about moving on to make a new start, Miss Rose. Small-town gossip can be too bothersome to bother fighting, and I'll have to allow your family left you with a hard row to hoe."

She didn't argue. He hadn't expected her to. He went on to say, "You're still young and pretty. You wouldn't be lying if you told the folks down the road apiece that you had no kin left for any of them to speculate on. You'll be free to settle down and start another family with mayhaps more luck next time."

She whirled on him, red-rimmed eyes blazing, demanding, "Are you out of your mind? Do you think I'd be mad enough to marry up and risk bringing another drooling idiot like Howard into this cruel world? I thought we'd just agreed it's *over,* all over. I'll never ever have to assure anyone that my leering baby brother is really harmless again! I'll never ever have anybody pointing me out as the sister who was shielding a sex fiend when the county wanted to put him away! I'll be *free,* free at last of pissed-in pants and sniggering laughter from behind lace curtains as I pass!"

Mrs. Forbes came back into her front parlor, nodding slightly at Longarm as she asked if they needed any more coffee. Neither of them had tasted her first servings of cake and coffee. So Longarm allowed he was just about through with his interview, and got to his feet.

As he helped Rose Burnside to her own feet, she acted confused and said she'd expected him to ask her more about her brother's alleged crime. He said, "I would if only I could get you to say he done it, Miss Rose. Since you seem so sure he never did, and since neither of us was there, I reckon it's a Mexican standoff betwixt us and I'll just have to go interview somebody else."

The coroner's wife shot him a grateful look and calmly told the girl, "They've loaded your brother's remains aboard the hearse, Miss Burnside. Speaking from some experience in such matters, if I were you I'd join them later at the funeral parlor."

But Rose Burnside barely excused herself and tore back through the house to chase after her kid brother's cut-up cadaver.

Mrs. Forbes sighed and said, "Poor thing. They won't even be able to compose his features until the rigor passes, hopefully in a few more hours. They say he was all the family she had. So I suppose she must have been very fond of him, despite the way he acted."

Longarm nodded soberly and replied, "I know that's what they say. Would you tell your husband and Nurse Calder I'll talk to them some more at the hearing this evening? I was about to leave on some late afternoon chores when I wound up talking to Miss Rose just now."

She said she'd be proud to, and showed Longarm out the front door. As he legged it toward the courthouse square, a familiar voice hailed him and he saw that printer from his boardinghouse, Preston, standing in a doorway with an older gent.

The gilt lettering on the plate-glass window to one side of them identified the establishment as the *Pawnee Junction Advertiser*. So Longarm crossed over to see if he could save himself some time at the library he'd been headed for.

Preston introduced him to his boss, the editor and publisher of the weekly paper. The older man, who said Longarm ought to just call him Jake, like everyone else, said they were sticking the last type for their Monday edition and asked if Longarm had any statement to make about his pending showdown with Two-Gun Porky Shaw.

To which Longarm could only reply, "I don't recall inviting Porky Shaw to any showdown. Are you saying he'd been going around telling folks the same?"

Jake of the *Advertiser* said, "No. A lot of others are. They're taking bets on the outcome at the Red Rooster—with you the favorite, I'm sure you'll be pleased to hear."

Longarm snorted in disgust and replied, "The hell you say! I'm a grown man, for Gawd's sake. I gave up meeting the class bully after school a long time ago."

Jake shrugged and replied in a knowing tone, "You may have grown up. But speak for yourself, Longarm. You're a stranger who's brought a rep to town, and many a town bully has never been able to pass on a chance like that just for the glory. But the way *we* have it, there's more than the usual glory involved. The way we have it, you crawfished Porky Shaw in public. You ran him out of the barbershop before he could get his shave and a haircut free. You called him a coward to his face and told him to fill his fist then and there if he didn't like it. He didn't like it. So he ran—caught off guard and not sure he ought to draw on a lawman, he's saying *now*."

"Now?" asked Longarm thoughtfully.

The younger printer he'd be supping with later, with any luck, said, "That was earlier, over in the Red Rooster. He's not there now. Some say he rode out to the Diamond B to rustle up some backing. Some say he's left for good. It ain't easy to get backing when the play calls for man-to-man with nobody hiding his face."

Old Jake sounded cheerful as hell, considering, when he chimed in. "Porky will never get any of his pals to shoot it out in broad day with a paid-up lawman. He's going to have to fight you fair and square, or maybe hide out until those Minute Men come at you in a bunch in the dark."

Longarm cocked a brow and demanded, "You mean *you* think Porky Shaw is tied in with those Minute Men too?"

The two newspapermen exchanged glances. Preston was the one who told him, "Thinking is one thing. Proving it would be a bitch. Even if we could, the sheriff is scared skinny of them and these plate-glass windows cost the earth!"

40

Chapter 6

He only had to ask directions once, and found the public library handy to their one schoolhouse near the square. The schoolhouse was closed for the summer. Longarm might have thought the library was as well, if he hadn't just had dinner with Miss Ellen Brent, who worked there. For the front door was locked and nobody came before he'd banged on it considerably.

When she did open up, the perky little brunette looked as if she might have just had to dress in a hurry. Her face was flushed and, had women been allowed to sweat when they were only supposed to glow, he'd have sworn she was sweating like hell inside that buttoned-up seersucker bodice.

But she seemed glad to see him, and as she let him inside her large one-room library, he saw no signs of the hay she'd been pitching or the gent she'd been screwing. She said she hadn't known she'd locked the fool front door after her when she'd come back from her noon dinner, and added with a laugh that she'd been wondering why business had seemed so slow. Longarm didn't ask how come she hadn't heard him or anybody else knocking. It was a lady's own business if she wanted to take a nap or play with herself in the back, as long as he wasn't paying her salary.

He asked if he could use her card index, and it was her turn to be discreet and not ask where a gent who talked so country had learned to scout up reading material in a hurry.

But she couldn't hold back totally once he'd selected a privately printed local history and a medical tome. She said he could carry them home to read without a regular library card, seeing he was the law, but asked him what he expected to find in those particular mighty tedious-sounding books.

Hefting the heavy textbook and lighter publication, Longarm explained, "I've found in my travels that there's almost always some proud member of a local founding family willing to pay some printer to run off a handsomely bound history of that family. You can't hardly brag on your own bunch being one of the dozen or less original land-grabbers without saying at least a few words, good or bad, *about* them. I see this here Remington Ramsay who sells lumber and bobwire seems to feel the noble outline of his own family tree is worth preserving for future generations. I ain't as interested in hardware as I am hardcase cattle barons who might rate a line or more in here."

She wrinkled her pert nose and said, "I don't see why even a snob like Bob Wire Rem would trouble himself with a history of a township less than five years old. That medical casebook you're holding is even newer. We just got it in a month or so ago."

Longarm said, "I noticed the publication date. That's how come I want to borrow it, ma'am. Them alienists who study the human brain are at it day and night. So it's possible somebody's noticed something new since Dr. Langdon Down's famous study of '66."

She looked surprised and asked, "Surely you're not investigating the murder of that Sunday school teacher in addition to the lynching of a federal prisoner, are you?"

To which he could only reply, "Looks like I'd better. For the one seemed to follow the other as the night does the day. Those so-called Minute Men could have been bent on aveng-

42

ing Miss Mildred Powell, like they said, or they could have been out to cover something else up. I keep telling the rough-justice bunch that once you take the law into your own hands you confuse law and order a heap.''

As he ticked his hat brim at her to be on his way, Ellen Brent took hold of his free sleeve and said, ''Wait! You can't dash off and leave me hanging, as if the last page of a thrilling romance was missing, just as I was getting to the end of it! I agree those night riders were awfully mean and that it would have been better to hold a trial and at least hear the idiot's side of the story before they hung him. But I don't see what anyone could hope to *cover up* by hanging him a little sooner. Are you suggesting they were holding the wrong man? Do you think it likely that a dying woman would accuse a harmless idiot when she had that chance, and only that chance, to name her attacker?''

Longarm shrugged and said, ''There's this old church song I'm sure the late Sunday school teacher must have known. It's called 'Farther Along' and advises us to just keep poking along down the straight and narrow until, sooner or later, we'll know more about it farther along. I do have my troubles with the straight and narrow, but I've sure known more about things farther along. So I try not to guess wild until I have me some solid facts to guess with. I'll be proud to tell you where I am farther along, Miss Ellen. Right now I have to do some reading, attend that coroner's inquest this evening, and with any luck, scout up some new sign to follow. What time do you turn in over to that boardinghouse we're both bedded down in?''

She blinked, dimpled, and said, ''I usually trim my lamp by nine or ten, unless I have a good book to read. But I have to be more discreet than *that*, Custis! It would never do for you to come sniffing around an unmarried lady's bedchamber after sunset!''

He hadn't been planning to. But he didn't want to hurt her feelings. So he said, ''I generally have me a smoke out on

43

the front porch before I turn in. I can't say what time that might be this evening. But if all else fails there's always breakfast, and if I've found anything out, I can walk you to work tomorrow, right?''

She said that sounded more prudent, as if she was expecting him to share some dreadful secret. She'd have really been pissed if he'd told her he hardly ever shared dreadful secrets with anybody. So he nodded as if in agreement and headed back to their boardinghouse.

He got there well before quitting time for the rest of her boarders. So he caught the Widow MacUlric crying fit to bust in her kitchen when he came in the back way.

She shied like a fawn and tried to pretend she'd only been singing to herself, of course. But he'd heard her sobs and seen the way she'd been standing, head down and elbows braced in either corner of her kitchen sink. The sink was filled to overflowing with pots, pans, and greasy suds. Long-arm hung up his hat and gun rig, rolled up his shirtsleeves, and quietly said, "I'll wash if you'll dry, provided you let me use some sand from your garden, ma'am. We got our pots and pans looking shiny-new with no more than sand and wood ashes in my army days. But no offense, the water out this way ain't soft enough for that naphtha soap you're using.''

For some reason, that really made her bawl, and the next he knew, she was stuck to the front of him, crying all over his shirt and vest as she blubbered, "I can't! I can't! There's just so much to do and so few hours in the day, Deputy Long!''

He said she could call him Custis as he held her in a brotherly way, patting her back as she shuddered and wept against him. He told her he'd just been talking with an Indian Agency official, and asked if she'd considered hiring just one Pawnee gal to help out with the less skilled chores for no more than room, board, and a few coins to rub together now and again.

Mavis MacUlric wet his shirt front some more with tears, spit, or snot, and confessed, "I can't even afford Arbuckle Brand coffee. I've figured my expenses to the bone and it's just no use. I simply can't keep up the payments and run this place as a boardinghouse on what I take in!"

He asked why she didn't just charge her boarders a tad more in that case, adding, "Three dollars a week ain't as much as I've seen many a boardinghouse charge in other parts, Miss Mavis."

She answered flatly, "I'm not competing with anyone in *other* parts. Three a week is the going price in Pawnee Junction. My few boarders could get room and board for that, or maybe less, from what I hear about one landlady with a bigger house and no mortgage payments hanging over her. Did I mention the county and township fees, speaking of expenses, and these . . . God . . . damned . . . pots and pans!"

He gently disengaged himself from her as he told her firmly, "You worry about rustling up a simple supper whilst I get to work on these dinner pots and pans. You wouldn't have so many to wash if you'd learn to cook army or cow-camp style. When you open a can of beans and set 'em in a pan of boiling water can and all, you wind up with your beans just as boiled and a pan you only have to wipe out with a vinegar-soaked rag from time to time. I can give you lots of tips on cooking, Miss Mavis. But right now I'd best go out and scoop me up some scouring sand, hear?"

There was no accounting for female moods. That got her to laughing like hell for some reason. Then she fussed and said it wasn't right to make a boarder help with housekeeping chores. So he told her nobody had even been able to *make* him wash pots and pans since he'd gotten out of the army.

As she simmered down and got to work side by side with him, once he'd shown her how clean garden dirt looked as soon as you rinsed all the worms out with a couple of changes of water, the young widow got less gloomy for the time being. As he stacked the first well-scoured pans to dry, she marveled, "You *do* know what you're doing! You say you were once a soldier, like my man Martin? He was a soldier in the war. He rode with Pope at the second Bull Run, and after he was well again, he rode against the Sioux out this way."

Longarm rubbed harder on the pan he was scouring as he asked in a mildly interested tone, "Do tell? From those Confederate war bonds you used to paper that one wall upstairs, I had the impression you might be Texas folks, no offense."

She hunkered down to haul out some baking potatoes as she sighed and said, "That was Martin for you, the poor dear. He grew up in Penn State, and I was the girl next door who waited for him while he won the war for us all. Martin MacUlric was never a lazy man. He had his points, and we were very happy until his poor generous heart gave out on him at an obscenely young age. But he was a man for dreaming, and so many of his dreams were . . . so dreamy. He bought those Confederate war bonds from another dreamer, or a confidence man, who was certain the South would rise again, or at least redeem those bonds at ten cents on the dollar."

Longarm said, "I may have met up with a similar investment-consulting gent a spell back. We called him Soapy Smith. I was the one who ran him out of Denver over another swindle he'd been pulling. Ten cents on the dollar and he only asked two bits, right?"

She sighed and began to wash the spuds she'd chosen in another pan he was going to have to wash if she didn't calm down. She said Martin MacUlric, owing steep payments on this house they'd just bought in a railroad town certain to boom, had been suckered worse with those high-face-value railroad bonds.

She said, "The story Martin was sold about those pretty pictures of choo-choo trains involved some tortured rehash of that awfully complicated Credit from Mobile eight or ten years back. Martin tried to explain it to me when they were talking about putting Vice President Colfax in jail, but to tell the truth, I couldn't make heads or tails of the scandalous mess!''

Longarm grimaced and replied, ''I doubt poor old Colfax or President Grant could have explained that mess sober. The investigation sniffed in vain in '72 and '73 for dirty deeds done early as '64, when Honest Abe was in the crow's nest and likely didn't know what they were doing either. You're not alone in finding that Credit Mobilier of America a can of worms indeed. You're saying your late husband invested in those Credit Mobilier of America bonds whilst he was in the service, ma'am?''

She sighed and said, ''No. He bought them out here eighteen months ago—at too big a discount to pass up, he said—from a railroad man with a drinking problem and some fairy tale about not having the time left to wait for them to mature.''

Longarm nodded knowingly and said, ''I hear that Credit Mobilier scandal left lots of investors with stocks and bonds worth more as wallpaper, ma'am. Took the railroads a long time to get over that crisis in confidence, and some say the country ain't quite over the Great Depression of the seventies yet. But at least you still have this property, and things are commencing to pick up again. We had us a wetter than usual greenup out this way, and the price of beef and other produce keeps rising.''

She sighed and said, ''Don't I know it! I just had to pay for the groceries you'll be eating tonight, thanks to your help as I was about to slash my wrists, you sweet man.''

He said, ''Aw, mush. This seems to be the last pan, and I have some reading to catch up on before I 'tend that coroner's hearing after supper. So why don't I carry these fool books upstairs and get out of your way?''

She assured him he wasn't in her way. But he figured she must have still been feeling tense because he heard her busting a china cup on the floor as he was headed up the stairs.

He found it too sunny and hot up in his hired room at that hour. He didn't want to carry the books back through the kitchen to the cooler backyard with the widow in such an uncertain mood. So he swung the casement all the way out and sat on the sill with one boot up to light a cheroot and leaf through both books, taking notes in pencil from time to time. Ellen Brent had been right about the family brag of the hardware man, which told him little he hadn't already guessed at. The township and surrounding range were divided sharply, but not in a serious feud, as far as one could tell while selling lumber and bobwire to both the original stockmen and more recent sodbusters. Longarm knew from his earlier trips up this way that there was just no way a homesteader with or without a lick of sense could plow enough of the higher sand-hill range to matter. Unless you farmed down in the lower and wider draws, where the water table rested on peat and clay, you were never going to raise a thing but windblown sand. The stockmen, on the other hand, had more use for the well-drained grassy rises than the often cold and swampy draws. So the stockmen and nester would likely get along a few more years in these parts before they had all that much to fight about.

The medical tome confirmed his guess that science was trying to keep up with unfortunates such as the late Bubble-head Burnside. They'd dug up more figures and studied more Mongoloids since Langdon Down's first description of the syndrome. That was what they called what Bubblehead had suffered—a syndrome.

There was nothing in the medical tome about crazy folks that offered any explanation as to why the Widow MacUlric was singing like a canary bird downstairs, for Gawd's sake.

Chapter 7

Pawnee Junction barely ran eight city blocks each way, but it was getting tedious to leg it in high summer. So after supper Longarm hired a chestnut gelding and a stock saddle from the livery next door to attend that coroner's hearing in style.

Seeing he had the time as well as a pony under him, he scouted those few parts of the small business district he wasn't too clear about on all sides of the courthouse square. It took less than ten minutes to circle more than once. He found Pawnee Junction about as tedious from any point of view. But he did take note of the chunky paint pony out front of Spaulding's Funeral Parlor and Furniture Shop when he saw it was sidesaddled. That had to be the famous Grassy, named by a half-wit and ridden by his sole survivor.

Another sidesaddled Indian pony, this one a buckskin, was tethered out front of the county courthouse along with many other horses. Longarm dismounted and half-hitched his own reins to the hitching rail. When he went inside, he wasn't surprised to spy Nurse Nancy Calder milling back through the main courtroom with the others in her tan riding habit. He drifted after her, admiring her rear view and the way the gloaming light from the windows along one side highlighted her thick taffy brown hair. It was a pure wonder how gals could look so much different from one another and still look swell. Nurse Calder was as tall as the Widow MacUlric, but built more like that brunette from the library and . . . It was best not to undress them any further in one's mind when one had matters of life and death to ponder.

As promised, the hearing was being held in a back room behind the judge's chambers and cloakroom. Doc Forbes and a half-dozen other gents were seated between the rear wall and a long table the county commission likely used for its own sessions at other times. Everyone else made do as best they could on folding chairs or standing in the larger space left in the crowded chamber. Longarm moved over to one corner to stand with his back wedged into it so he could just worry about the hearing. Nurse Calder took a seat she was offered down at one end of the panel. The rest of the crowd was dressed mostly cow or corn, with reporters from both the *Advertiser* and rival *Monitor* obvious amid the handful of townsmen. Longarm noticed they hadn't bunched up in sullen clumps the way men did in a community at feud. That bragging local history by the hardware man had said all original white settlers had depended on one another when Dull Knife and his Cheyenne were scaring western Nebraska just a few autumns back.

Doc Forbes finally banged on the table for silence and declared, "This hearing has been called to decide the causes of two deaths. That of the late David Loman, alias Dancing Dave, and Howard Burnside, who was better known as Bubblehead. This shouldn't take long because, with the help of Nurse Calder yonder, I autopsied both those boys this very afternoon."

He picked up some papers as if to read them, decided the technical terms would only confuse his fellow panelists, and declared, "I can sum it up best by saying they both died instantaneously from the same trauma. Seriously broken necks with severed spinal columns.''

A cowhand seated near the back joyfully volunteered, ''They say that'll happen ever time when you tie a rope around a rascal's neck and shove him off a railroad trestle.''

Doc Forbes silenced the laughter with a severe look and told them all, ''We have to word our official report soberly. How does manslaughter at the hands of person or persons unknown strike the rest of you?''

There came a murmur of agreement from both the panel and their audience. So Longarm called out, ''Manslaughter my Aunty Fanny! When you set out alone or in a bunch with the avowed intention of killing somebody, and then you kill not one but two, the legal definition of your crime is premeditated murder in the first degree!''

Dod Forbes said that sounded fair. But another man on the panel, who looked like he and Buffalo Bill bought their outfits at the same shops, protested, ''Hold on. The Minute Men ain't murderers. I'll allow they might have been rougher than they needed to be on that one train robber the other night. But they had just cause to be het up about the fiendish ravaged murder of that poor little Sunday school gal!''

The agreement was louder this time. As it died down a fussy-dressed gent wearing his glasses with a string on them cleared his throat and fussed, ''We held our hearing on the death of Mildred Powell the day before yesterday. I see no reason to rehash it. We agreed on those findings, and the grand jury surely would have indicted that half-wit if the Minute Men hadn't taken the law into their own hands.''

''Three cheers for the Minute Men!'' yelled another cowhand, to be seconded by a townsman, who called, ''Saved the grand jury a meeting and Lord knows what it might have cost the taxpayers to go on guarding and feeding that ravenous half-wit!''

Nurse Calder rose to her five-foot-six or so and snapped, ''You gentlemen are the ones who sound like half-wits!

Thanks to the murder of Howard Burnside, we'll never really know what happened the other day in the basement of First Calvinist!''

The older man dressed like Buffalo Bill or a mighty well-paid top hand looked up at her, surprised, and said, ''We know what happened to Miss Mildred, Nurse Calder. She told Nick Olsen and Rafe Jennings who'd just ravaged her and left her for dead when they found her bleeding to death on the cement floor down yonder!''

Nurse Calder sniffed and said, ''Dr. Forbes let me read all that. Then I assisted him in the examination of your accused rapist. Howard Burnside had the mind and sex drive of a pre-school child. He had the sex organs to go with them, and there was no indication she'd been raped in Mildred Powell's autopsy report!''

A tall young man wearing a low-crowned Stetson rose to his feet in the crowd and called out, ''Hold on, there, ma'am. I'd be Rafe Jennings and I was holding Miss Mildred's head on my knee, trying to help her breathe, as she told me and Nick Olsen yonder she'd been raped and stabbed by old Bubblehead—or Howard as *she* called him.''

The taffy-headed gal in tan shrugged and replied simply, ''She was confused, or you heard her wrong. It's *possible* for a woman to have sex with a man without retaining any, ah, results in her vagina. But even if he'd been wearing a condom, that immature Mongoloid idiot was simply not man enough to rape anybody!''

The lout who'd raised a cheer for the Minute Men laughed lewdly and asked, ''Did you take a yardstick to both them dead boys, ma'am? Is that true about hanged men having hard-ons after they're dead?''

More than one man present laughed uncomfortably. But if the cool-eyed Nancy Calder was embarrassed, she failed to show it. Staring right at the crude cowhand, she sweetly replied, ''You might or might not defecate or ejaculate as you died instantly with a severed spinal column. I can assure you they'd have dropped real loads and shot their wads if you'd strangled them slowly."

The cowhand protested, "Hold on. Don't you go saying it was *my* notion to kill them boys last night!"

That really got the crowd to buzzing. Doc Forbes pounded the table and declared them both out of order. So Nurse Calder sat back down.

That allowed the panel to jaw back and forth about crossing some Ts or dotting an occasional I. In the end they decided to send a bill of John Doe indictments on to the county prosecutor and let him worry about it.

As the hearing was declared over and everyone tried to get over to the Red Rooster at once, Longarm stayed put in his corner until, sure enough, Nurse Nancy Calder moved along one wall toward him, looking sheepish as she nodded and said, "You're right. I should have kept my big mouth shut. I think I was called up here to verify the sex-mad rages of Mongoloid idiots. I'm sorry if I let everyone down, but at least I have that brain to carry back to the agency with me, if only I can get permission from the next of kin. I'm not sure Dr. Forbes likes me anymore."

Longarm said, "Just stay put a minute and let the stampede die down, ma'am. Doc Forbes is all right. He's just a small-town sawbones depending on the county machine for the difference betwixt living well and struggling. I don't think he'd lie deliberately. I just heard one witness testify the dead gal accused that Burnside boy. As to that brain you two took out of his odd-shaped skull this afternoon, I might be able to help you out there. His sister, Miss Rose, is sitting wake on him over to the funeral parlor. Let me do the talking and we might be able to get her permission."

He explained about his earlier conversation with the dead boy's next of kin. She agreed it was worth a try, and allowed a written statement from a peace officer, confirming an oral agreement, would cover her with the Bureau of Indian Affairs if push ever came to shove.

As they followed the last of the crowd outside, the sun was all the way down and the western sky was painted red and gold where it wasn't already purple. So the lighting was a tad tricky as they moved around to where they'd tethered their mounts. But Longarm made it an even half-dozen men blocking their paths, all but one under broad-brimmed hats, with the odd one a derby.

Getting right to the point, one of them announced, "We don't hold with trash-talking sluts coming here to accuse our pals of lying, you Indian-loving slut!"

Longarm moved the gal out of his line of fire as he quietly but firmly declared, "You say that one more time or call this lady one more name and I am going to clean your plow, cowboy!"

"You think you're big enough?" jeered another voice from the coyote pack.

Longarm said, "You'd best mount up and go on home after the doc, Nurse Calder. We might be holding another coroner's hearing here directly."

Then another party loomed out of the darkness to declare in a no-nonsense tone, "That'll be enough for tonight, boys. Go on home, Tom. You too, Latigo. I mean it, and we all know what happens if I have to repeat myself!"

It seemed to work. As the surly crowd dispersed without a lick of back-sass, Longarm nodded knowingly at the pewter badge worn by the darkly dressed figure who'd come to their rescue.

Longarm started to introduce the nurse and himself. The sardonic lawman in black said, "I know who you two are and you both make me nervous. I'd be Pronto Cross, the town marshal. I thought me and Sheriff Wigan had a gentleman's agreement. I don't concern myself with anything that might take place a furlong outside of town, and in return nobody rides at full gallop or discharges his firearms *in* town."

Longarm nodded soberly and said, "I have heard tell of a

54

town-tamer called Pronto Cross. They tell me he blew a wild cowboy off his pony when he rode it through a schoolyard down Kansas way.''

Pronto Cross shrugged modestly and replied, ''School was in session and he'd been warned. When people pay you to preserve law and order in a town, you're supposed to preserve law and order. No offense, but neither of you federal employees are making my job any easier in Pawnee Junction!''

Nurse Calder said, ''I was just about to leave! They told me the *Pawnee* were savages when I signed up to work out this way! I've yet to meet any Indian who openly admired cowardly killers who gang up on women!''

Pronto Cross laughed softly and assured her, ''Nobody in that bunch was a Minute Man, ma'am. They were just young jaspers who forgot the way we expect 'em to act in town.''

Longarm nodded grimly and said, ''I'd been wondering how come your county sheriff led those two prisoners out back to the mob instead of making a stand inside brick walls. You and your town deputies would have had to come to help if the shooting had started within the town boundaries. Is it safe to assume Sheriff Wigan knows all the Minute Men on a first-name basis too?''

Pronto Cross answered innocently, ''Most everyone in the county can name most everyone else, if he cares to. You must have noticed by now that nobody cares to. Do us all a favor, Longarm. Wind it up before anyone else gets hurt. I've passed the word to leave you alone until you leave. I don't know how long I can hold them off. I'd like to do more for you, but it's an election year and a man can only do so much before he has to look out for his own skin, if you follow my meaning.''

Longarm said, ''I follow your meaning. Come on, Nurse Calder, we'll go see about that permission you need from Rose Burnside and I'll ride you partway back to the agency.''

Pronto Cross nodded agreeably and said, ''I'm glad you

both see it my way. What's done is done and there's no sense hanging around where you just ain't wanted, right?''

Longarm just took the gal by one elbow and led her around the rumps of their ponies. There were some questions that deserved polite answers. There were others that were just too dumb to bother with.

Chapter 8

They were shown in to find Rose Burnside seated stiffly near the foot of her brother's closed coffin of mahogany-stained pine with cast-iron handles. The velveteen-draped viewing chamber was candlelit mighty poorly. So it was hard to read the gal's expression when Longarm introduced the Indian Agency nurse to her and added, "If it's of any comfort to you, Miss Rose, Nurse Calder and me just now found out your brother wasn't an idiot. He was an imbecile. That's way smarter than an idiot, and I have even better news for you."

Both gals seemed interested as he continued. "When Dr. Langdon Down made his first serious studies of your brother's syndrome, as you describe it scientifically, he was starting from scratch with rough data. Down's description of what earlier docs had written off more cruelly was a vast improvement, of course. He freed all those poor women of nasty suspicions about their visits to the Chinese laundry, and pointed out that real Mongolians were just about as smart as anyone else, without pinkies that turned in or thicker tongues than most. But the doc jumped to some hasty conclusions of his own, starting with calling the condition Mongoloid idiocy. More recent studies have shown a greater

57

number of such odd-looking children, no offense, are smarter than true idiots, which are baby-brained. Most are imbeciles, meaning they think at about the level of a six-or eight-year-old, with some of them even smarter, able to read, write, and do sums at a sixth-grade level.''

He let that sink in, then told her gently, ''We'll never be able to ask your brother to take any written tests, of course. But it would tell us more about him and others like him if you'd let Nurse Calder here take some, ah, tissue samples back to her clinic down to the Pawnee Agency.''

Rose shook her head and said, ''I'll not have anyone poking about inside Howard again. I'm sure the undertakers did their best this evening. But he already looks as if he's been stuffed!''

That wasn't such a bad description when you studied on it. But Longarm said, ''Nobody wants to disturb his remains again, Miss Rose. They, ah, did all they had to to his innards this afternoon. I was there, and you have my word nobody did or said anything disrespectful of you or your family. Nurse Calder just spoke up for your brother at the coroner's hearing, as a matter of fact. She said right out she didn't think he did half the things they say he did to that Sunday school gal. She wouldn't have been able to offer such an opinion if she and Doc Forbes hadn't sort of . . . poked around at him.''

Rose looked up hopefully at the bigger gal, who nodded soberly and said, ''Whatever happened, I can't see how your brother could have raped anybody.''

Rose said, ''I was wondering about that. He never seemed to take any interest in such matters, even when neighborhood kids came by to watch the stock going at it. You see, swine are built sort of odd and, well . . .''

''Nurse Calder needs your permission to study some more on what made your brother tick,'' Longarm said. ''It's important to have somebody study and write things down. For example, we know from more recent studies that your broth-

58

er's syndrome doesn't run in the family, as you said you feared. The reason you and your other brother were born normal to the same mother is that Mongolism seems to be little more than a game of chance, with one out of, say, five hundred mothers losing out."

Nurse Calder showed she'd been keeping up with the literature by cautiously adding, "Older women who've been ill seem to run a higher risk of bearing a Mongoloid child. Nobody knows why *any* woman might give birth to such a child. But Custis is right about the odds, and it's very common to see one such child among a large family of normal brothers and sisters."

"*They* usually spoil the funnier-looking kid brothers or sisters," Longarm volunteered. As the nurse nodded he went on. "Like you can say from your own experience, that particular breed of half-wit tends to be lovable as well as embarrassing. They like to play, seldom play rough, and hardly ever raise a fuss. But why go on about such family problems when the odds are you'll never have to worry about anything like that again, Miss Rose?"

The small gal in black gasped, "Oh, thank you! Thank you for telling me that! I've been sitting her and sitting here, knowing how my poor mamma must have felt when she ran off that way, and, oh, I do so hope you're not just saying that to make me feel better!"

Longarm swore they weren't, and brought up the delicate matter of pickle jars again. She told them they could keep anything they'd ever found in her unfortunate brother's cadaver for all *she* cared, and Longarm got Nurse Calder out of there before she could change her mind.

It was really getting dark outside by then. Nancy Calder suddenly grabbed hold of Longarm's vest and gave him a sisterly peck on one cheek before she said, "That was very sweet of you, Custis. You do have a way with women, for a man who can be so stern with a half-dozen men at a time!"

He said, "Aw, mush. I'm as nice to anybody as their manners call for. I never lied to anybody just now. I read most everything I told her in this book I borrowed from the library this afternoon. Where's that poor boy's brain right now, over to the Forbes house?''

She demurely replied, ''In my saddlebag. I don't have to go back to say my good-byes to anyone in this horrid town. I know poor Dr. Forbes has to pay attention to the side his bread is buttered on. But I still feel used and abused. He wanted me to confirm that poor idiot—or, all right, imbecile—as a frothing-at-the-mouth sex maniac! Do you want to know what *I* think, Custis? I think those two cowboys found her alone, raped her and stabbed her, then lied about her telling them the village idiot had done it!''

He said, ''The thought had crossed my mind. Let's mount up and get you out of town before anybody *else* hears you! How far a ride are we talking about, Miss Nancy?''

She said, ''Eight hours each way. I'd hardly put a pal through sixteen hours in the saddle. So why don't you just ride me down to where I leave the railroad service trace to follow an old buffalo trail I know. If nobody is ghosting after us that far south, I doubt I'll have anything to worry about from there on to the agency.''

That made sense, and he said it did as he helped her up aboard her sidesaddle. He mounted the chestnut and, at his suggestion, they rode out of town at a walk, due east, by crossing the tracks and following the evening star instead of any trail of man or beast.

It was easy to do so in the Sand Hill Country, where the short-grass range formed an open sea of gentle swells. He was hoping she might not ask why they were leaving town so strangely. But he'd already noticed she had a suspicious mind. So he wasn't too surprised when she flatly said, ''If that bunch the town marshal dispersed are laying for us, they'll be set up along the southbound rails and service trace.''

It had been a statement rather than a question. He still

nodded and said, "I don't know if anyone's after us or not. But it's been my sad experience that you really hate yourself when you ride into an ambush you could have avoided easy."

She asked, "Wouldn't it prove my point if somebody tried to kill me, Custis? You saw how angry some of them were back at the hearing when I implied Howard Burnside hadn't ever raped that girl. They say she was pretty, and boys will be boys. But she was a Sunday school teacher, and so, when she spurned their advances . . ."

"Doc Forbes said *nobody* left any, ah, evidence in her," Longarm declared, adding, "*One* drunken country boy could do most anything, with or without brains and some vulcanized protection. It would be tougher to get a pal to go along with such rough wooing, and that one kid at the meeting seemed sort of simple. I mean, just saying you were never there and don't know anything takes a less devious brain than pinning it on even a half-wit. You and me can't be the only ones who'd ever wonder about anyone that simple acting so dirty."

He figured they were far enough out to swing south in line with her more predictable route to her agency. The idea was to ride wide enough to avoid an ambush, but close enough to make out any signs of such a setup. As they walked their mounts over a grassy rise in the cool evening breeze from the west, the agency gal declared, "If we spot anyone laying for us, it will mean I was right about that lynch mob as well. Can't you see that they lynched those two innocent boys to cover up the crimes of Nick Olsen and Rafe Jennings?"

To which he could only reply, "Dancing Dave wasn't all that innocent, and they were likely convinced of the half-wit's guilt as well. I try not to turn a game of checkers into a fancy chess game unless I have to, Miss Nancy. The murder of Mildred Powell was local, with a paid-up county coroner and sheriff's department to investigate it. The murder of Bubblehead Burnside falls on the same side of their fence and, hardcased as it may seem, they don't pay me to administer justice in cases where it ain't my chore. The murder of a federal want and a possibly valuable government witness is the one and only crime I can't get out of investigating. It doesn't matter to my home office whether that mob had just cause to lynch one of their own. They lynched a man I had first dibs on. So that's the matter before the house as far as I'm concerned.''

She seemed to feel that wasn't fair. They rode on, and then on some more, until they were sure they were well south of the trestle the mob had used to murder Loman and Burnside. At Longarm's suggestion they swung over to the bare ruts of the service trace running in line with the tracks and telegraph poles. The surer footing and safer distance from town allowed them to lope their ponies downslope, walk them up slope, and trot along the flatter stretches, making better time but enjoying less conversation, of course.

So she'd saved up a whole bushel of new theories about recent events back in Pawnee Junction by the time he called a trail break in a watered draw and got down to light up as the ponies lowered their muzzles to the tea-colored peat water. As he helped Nancy down she said, ''I just thought of something. What if there was yet a third party, say a depraved church organist, who stabbed her when she said no to his unwelcome advances?''

He laughed and said, ''Now you're really talking like Mr. Edgar Allan Poe, no offense! How do you like this giant ape coming down from the belfry to catch the poor gal alone in the cellar? That's how come she told those cowboys she'd been attacked and stabbed by old Howard when they came running to see what she was screaming about. Howard was the name of this sex-mad ape who lives up in the belfry, see?''

She sat on the grassy slope and cast her hat aside to prop her weight on one hip and elbow as she laughed wryly and told him he was no fun. She said, ''In those stories the criminal is always very tricky and turns out to be the last person anyone suspected!''

He sat down beside her, getting rid of his own hat to cool his brow as he enjoyed his cheroot. He said, ''You'd be surprised how few great engineers and inventors we have locked up in prison, ma'am. If the ones who killed my particular prisoner had been as smart as, say, that ape in the belfry you prefer, they'd have never lynched Dancing Dave to begin with. *He* wouldn't have been able to say who hung an imbecile he didn't know. Nobody back there is half as clever as he thinks. Lynch law is stupid and brutal, indulged in by stupid and brutal bullies.''

She asked, ''How come you can't seem to pin anything on anybody then?''

He said, ''Nobody *wants* me to. Just a few short years ago this was Indian country, buffalo range disputed by Cheyenne and Pawnee. So the first settlers took to depending more on one another than, say, the far-off state troopers or even more remote army.''

He took a thoughtful drag and added, ''Outfits like those mining camp vigilance committees or range regulators down New Mexico way start out with good enough intentions. Some say the KKK filled a need that many felt no army of occupation was able to satisfy, at least at first. The trouble with outfits such as those Minute Men is that they don't disband once they've finished the chores they were set up for. General Nathan Bedford Forrest in the flesh ordered his Ku Klux Klan to disband in 1869, having done all it had been meant to do when they organized right after the war. But some old boys just never got over the thrill of dressing up like a spook and carrying on as if it was always going to be Halloween.''

He blew smoke out both nostrils and grumbled, ''Those fool Minute Men have a town law and a county sheriff they voted in *themselves*. I'll never in this life understand what makes some enjoy themselves so much when they get the chance to hurt others."

She stared thoughtfully his way without really being able to see him as she murmured, "You were pretty scary when those boys insulted me back there, Custis."

He shrugged and said, "I was too scared of them to enjoy myself. I reckon I can hold my own in a fight if I have to, and this job of mine makes me have to now and again. But I'll be switched if I can see why anybody would want to get all hot and bothered when they had no call to!"

She sighed and lay back on the dry grass as she said, "Speak for yourself. Picking on people is one thing. Getting hot and bothered can be another. How far would you say we've made it from that awful town, Custis?"

He said, "Seven or eight miles. With nobody following unless I've gone deaf. Give those tethered ponies a few more minutes rest and we can have you home well before cock's crow."

Her voice sounded oddly husky as she softly replied, "I told you I didn't want you to ride me all the way back to the agency. How would it look to everyone if I rode out of the wee small hours with a good-looking brute like you? This is as far as I want you to go with me, Custis. On horseback, I mean."

He said, "I can take a hint. Might my livery pony and me have your permission to just stay put until you're ready to ride on, ma'am?"

She laughed wickedly and replied, "You're dense as brick when it comes to taking a hint, you big silly! How on earth did you ever get your reputation as a range-riding Romeo with such prim and proper ways?"

He rolled half atop her and kissed her before he shyly confessed, with his free hand on one heroic breast, "Like most men, I'd rather miss out than look like a fool. But seeing you've asked, I wouldn't want you to take me for a sissy. So Powder River and let her buck, you demurely hinting thing!"

Chapter 9

Longarm had noticed on previous nude occasions under moonlight that gals with some medical background tended to take charge in a manner some men found unsettling. But Longarm seldom had trouble keeping it up when the gal was at all good-looking and seemed at all interested. When old Nancy got on top, weight balanced on her heels, to clamp down tight and bounce her hips up and down with her powerful thighs, he knew she was trying to be a real pal. So he got a hand down between them to tickle her fancy as she milked on his old organ-grinder with her ring-dang-doo.

She gasped, "Oh, yes, that feels grand and you really *are* a range-riding Romeo. But who ever taught you to masturbate a girl so girlishly?"

He laughed up at her. "A girl, of course. *You* all need some instructions to jerk a boy off boyishly. Men and women deserve someone better than each other, but at least we have the advantage over our ancestors up in the trees. We can compare notes as we go at it. So we don't have to be all frustrated in Professor Darwin's squirrel cage unless we're too shy to talk dirty to one another."

She laughed and said, "Roll me over and talk dirty to me

some more while I come. You're driving me crazy this way!''

So he did, made her come first, then enjoyed her his own way with one of her knees hooked over each of his stiff elbows.

After he'd ejaculated in her, touching bottom, Nancy gasped, ''I felt that! It felt good! But I'm glad you're not one of those poetic souls who moon about mingled mutual orgasms! What was that you said about those theories of Charles Darwin, dear? Has he written anything explaining why male and female sex organs were designed by what I've always suspected of being a committee of fiends with a view to driving most women mad with frustration?''

Longarm rolled off her to rope across the grass for a smoke and a light as he replied, ''Old Darwin only wrote that his evolving by selection favors critters who screw more because they're most likely to outbreed and crowd out their calmer cousins. It was this gal I know, embalming dead folks of all ages and local reps, who came up with a grim theory that the two sexes are built to maximize more screwing than satisfaction.''

He rolled back alongside her to light up as she snuggled closer and commenced to toy with what she'd just satisfied a lot—for the moment. He offered her a drag on the cheroot as he explained, ''Say you had two bands of smart baboons roaming the same sort of range. Say one bunch was content to act lovey-dovey as Darby and Joan, with every couple enjoying it mutually every time they got around to it, which might not be as often because nobody thinks as much about their sweet tooth in a chocolate shop.''

She purred, ''You mean they could just screw any time they felt like it, with nobody having to make any extra effort? It sounds divine!''

What she was doing to him felt swell too. He took a drag on their mutual smoke and said, ''I'm sure there must have been such screwings back when the living was easy under the fruit trees we come down out of. There are still happy couples, and every now and again you meet a lady who can just lay back and enjoy it.''

"You brute!" she snapped, gripping him harder where it felt good. "Are you suggesting I'm frigid?"

To which he sincerely replied, with some tweaking on his own part, "Not hardly. We *could* have said adios with a handshake. I only meant to say that, the way males and females are built, it takes way more time and effort for most gals to come, which takes us to our second, less satisfied, bunch of baboons. Say it's tougher for a he to satisfy a she, and what you wind up with is a series of drawn-out orgies, like the Romans used to hold, no doubt because they just couldn't get all they needed to calm down either."

She said, "Oh, dear, I'm starting to see what you mean! Thanks to my medical training I do take precautions. But there's no telling how many kids I'd have had by this time if I hadn't! You must have noticed how warm-natured I am, and I've been that way ever since I found out how good it could feel if only you did it long enough, often enough. You and Charles Darwin feel, in sum, that evolution has favored men who come free and easy, and women who don't, because that's the combination that leads to the most fornication?"

He snubbed out the cheroot and rolled back on top to insert all she'd inspired where it might do them the most good as he assured her, "I'm glad. Screwing scientifically is interesting, and I ain't sure a gal that came as easy as a man would be all that exciting. I suspect the challenge and variety you more complicated gals present must tie in with our hunting instincts. Stay-at-homes who never cared what lay over the next hill, or how that redhead down the valley screwed, couldn't have done all that much to extend human knowledge."

She gasped, "Ooh, that's a very interesting angle! But seeing we seem to enjoy being so frank about fornication, as a most refreshing change would you mind if I suggested some really scientific research?''

He said he was game for anything that didn't leave scars. So she confessed she'd always wanted to try servicing a man as a whore with medical training might, concentrating on nothing but pleasing him until he could come and repay the favors in the same way, playing her flesh as a skilled musician plays his instrument.

He laughed and said, ''Well, I've never tried to screw a fiddle and play pretty tunes on it at the same time. But I reckon I can try, and I want to make you come first.''

So she dared him to try, and he withdrew to kneel over her naked body in the moonlight and proceed, kissing and fondling her all over in a manner Queen Victoria might have found shocking, if not inspiring. He'd heard those royal folks got their underlings to pamper the hell out of them, and it was only a matter of degree from licking a royal foot to licking anywhere they might want you to.

Nancy gasped that he was making her feel like a spoiled gypsy queen. So he suspected old John Brown, Victoria's burly butler who put her to bed every night, likely knew one or two things about getting old gals hot. It was funny, because you usually thought of pimps and those Frenchmen that rich women hired when you thought about making a gal come without pleasuring your ownself at the same time. But as he got her to gasping for air and gushing with passion while he sort of played her like a violin, he felt the way a top hand could feel about mastering a bronc without having to come in the saddle. When he got *her* to come, and then come some more as she begged him to fiddle faster, he was proud of his self-control. Not many men could have held back at a time like that, even with a gal who was not as pretty. But he did, and then it was his turn and he was glad he had. For even though he'd already had her the old-fashioned way, she made him come three more times in ways that could have gotten the two of them thrown in jail in more states than one.

They wound up more naturally, like old pals, in the end. But neither felt like doing more than letting it soak inside her as she hugged him naturally with her bare arms and legs.

After a while in that position, she sighed and said, "Gee, I wish it wouldn't get me fired if I were to bring you back to the agency with me for at least a year!"

He kissed her and pointed out, "I doubt we'd feel like this for more than a month. That's how come they call it the honeymoon. Evolution's always favored the gals who nag men to go out and bring back a side of mammoth meat. But I reckon I could ride on a few more trail breaks with you, honey."

She sighed and said, "Lord knows when I'd ever get home at that rate. Please don't feel hurt, but I think we'd better quit while we don't want to, Custis. You're so right about the way lovers turn on one another after the honeymoon is over, and I want to remember you this way, as an adorable brute with a streak of gallantry and just about the nicest cock I've ever had in there. Could you move it some more before we part, just for old time's sake?"

He could and he did. Most men would have, including whoever she'd meant when she'd said "just about."

Her point about not waiting until everyone was completely sated was well taken, and well understood by every tumble-weed gent with love-'em-and-leave-'em tendencies. He came in her one more time—it seemed to take forever and left him wondering if it had been worth that much of an effort—and then it was time to put on their duds and act grown-up again. So they did, and parted with a kiss they could have gotten away with in public before they mounted up and rode their separate ways.

It was well after midnight, Lord love her rollicking rump, by the time Longarm headed back to Pawnee Junction alone. This time he walked his pony more and stayed closer to the railroad, pausing under that trestle to scout, without finding any sign he could use against anyone. You could only ride so many ponies around in circles before there wasn't any particular pattern left.

As he rode on north along the service trace with the wires above him humming in the dry night winds, he heard a far-off rumble and glanced up thoughtfully.

There wasn't a cloud in a sky so clear it seemed you might be able to scoop stars with your hat if you stood tall enough in the stirrups.

"Gunplay? At going on three in the morning?" he asked his chestnut livery mount in a puzzled tone. The gelding didn't act as if he'd even heard the far-off fusillade. Critters were better at judging how far off a night noise came from. They seldom spooked when it wasn't as close as a bigger beast could charge flat out. That was doubtless how come human beings invented wheels and such. They kept thinking about things they couldn't figure easy. As he rode on toward the once-more-quiet town, he decided some drunk had shot up the sky on his way home from the Red Rooster. Marshal Pronto Cross wouldn't put up with much more noise than Longarm had just heard. The noisy cuss would be locked up or long gone by the time Longarm could make it on into town. So he decided it wasn't his row to hoe.

Longarm wasn't sure what Western Union and Billy Vail would tell him he was supposed to hoe come morning. On the face of it, their federal prisoner could be said to have died on them by accident when those Minute Men avenged a purely local crime. Billy Vail wouldn't like it. Longarm didn't like it. But there was only so much money and man hours to be spent on all the injustices of an unjust world, and nobody expected them to find Captain Kidd's treasure or put a stop to child labor and patent medicine either. A whole township covering up for the rough justice of a lynch mob deserved such rough justice as they were likely to wind up with, and meanwhile, there was a new stenography gal at the Denver Federal Building who didn't know a soul in town, so what the hell.

As he saw the winking lights of Pawnee Junction ahead, he wondered why. It was after three in the morning. So why should so many folks be up at this hour?

He rode on in, heading first for the livery next door to his boardinghouse, but then swinging up towards the brighter lights between the railroad stop and Courthouse Square as he spotted more signs of action up that way.

As he walked his mount around a corner, he saw other ponies tethered out front of the Red Rooster, with bright lamplight spilling out across the plank walk from the doorway. He patted the neck of his hired chestnut and said, "This must be the place. Must be something going on if they're this busy at this hour."

He dismounted out front, tethered the chestnut handy to a watering trough, and strode across the plank walk to part the batwing doors and step into the noisy glare.

The hulking Porky Shaw was holding court at the bar, surrounded by admirers dressed town, corn, and cow as he raised his beer schooner to crow, "Here's to Longarm, who met his match! We drink to his dead meat! So down the hatch!"

Then he spied Longarm standing in the doorway with a thin bemused smile, and let go of the beer schooner to go for his guns as he screamed like an old maid who'd just found a man under her bed after all!

Porky was fast, and his side arms were riding side-draw in waxed leather. So he got his right-hand gun out first, and worse yet, it was double-action. But as he got off the first shot, it carried wide to spang a long splinter out of the door-jamb to Longarm's left as the cooler lawman was cross-drawing and aiming cooler. Then a .44-40 slug hit Porky dead center to stagger him back against the bar. He shot another round of .45-28 into the sawdust between them, and then fell flat on his face with a sad little sigh and a mighty

71

thud, still breathing but not long for this world, from the sounds he was making.

Longarm had already slid along the front wall to cover everyone politely from a corner as he calmly asked, "Would somebody please tell me why I just had to do that?"

That older man who dressed like Buffalo Bill's rich uncle rose from the corner table he'd been seated at with others to call out, "Porky was just telling us you were dead, Longarm. He'd only *hinted* he might have had something to do with your demise. But you can see from the way he just acted that he thought you had just cause to be vexed with him."

Longarm had just allowed he'd been vexed with Porky Shaw *before* the beefy bully had killed him when Marshal Pronto Cross and two of his town roundsmen came in to throw down on Longarm.

The barkeep called out helpfully, "Porky drew first, Marshal. Old Porky and those four, Baldy, Lefty, Riley, and Checkers, were with him. They'd just told everyone Longarm had been gunned by the Minute Men, for insulting them, when Longarm yonder came through that very door lively enough. Nobody but Porky drew on Longarm. You can see what a dumb move that was."

Pronto Cross moved over for a better look at the downed two-gun man as he announced for one and all, "One can see why Porky might have been taken aback. We just now came from the Widow MacUlric's. Porky or somebody just as mean shot up the front of that old frame considerable. They must have known which room our visitor from Denver had hired. It was a good thing for him he wasn't in that bed upstairs when somebody stepped up on the porch and kicked in the front door to fire up into the ceiling with at least two pistols and a Greener. For they surely shot the liver and lights out of that there empty mattress!"

Chapter 10

Porky Shaw had gurgled his last and Pronto Cross had questioned everyone in the Red Rooster by the time Doc Forbes arrived to roll the two-gun man over, pronounced him dead, and declare that there'd be another coroner's hearing that afternoon. Nobody there disputed his right to bill the county for another medical examination whether there was anything mysterious about the cause of death or not.

Joining Longarm at the bar for a mighty early drink, Doc Forbes asked if he knew where Nurse Calder had gone off to. When Longarm said he was almost certain she'd headed back to the Pawnee Agency, which was the simple truth no matter how anyone took it, Doc Forbes said it was just as well, explaining, "She's right handy with a bone saw, but for no more than a practical nurse she seems inclined to grab the bit in her teeth and boss us mere menfolk around."

Longarm said he'd noticed that, and added, "You don't need Porky's brains for anything, do you? I'm pretty sure I hit him just over the heart with my one round. He came way closer to a head shot, albeit he aimed a mite wide."

Forbes said he'd noticed the doorjamb, and agreed there seemed no good reason to open the fat man's skull because

73

they'd already established you couldn't tell how stupid a gent might have been just by gazing upon his dead brains.

Pronto Cross came to join them, saying, "All four of the old boys Porky was drinking with at the last have excuses for where they were when it appears Porky shot up that boardinghouse across town on his own and woke everybody up."

Longarm said, "I thought you said somebody tried to blast me out of bed with a Greener shotgun. So where is it and who might have been packing it?"

The town marshal shrugged and said, "Porky came over *here* alone, just as they were swamping up and laying new sawdust. What if some sidekick tore off into the dark with that Greener ten-gauge whilst a man who might have been more suspect came over here to establish an alibi."

"Or a brag," Longarm pointed out, reaching for his own beer as he added, "Porky was toasting my memory when I came through yonder door and inspired him to slap leather. He must have thought I lived through their fusillade by a whisker and knew who'd been shooting up through the floorboards at me. I'm always getting into fights with assholes saddled by a guilty conscience. More than once I've been credited with more smarts than I really had when some crook started up with me instead of leaving me the hell alone and just letting me ride on."

Pronto signaled the weary-looking barkeep for a morning beer as well, saying, "I follow your drift. Porky never would have had to crawfish at the barbershop if he'd only kept his big mouth shut. Is it safe for us to assume you'd have left town on your own and saved Porky the sad results of not just waiting you out?"

Longarm said, "That's about the size of it. I'm waiting on a wire from my boss, Marshal Billy Vail, before I can say for certain when I'll be leaving. I don't know how deep he might want me to dig into the lynching of that one federal prisoner. On the surface it seems highly unlikely members of his old gang had anything to do with his death, and we all know how tedious it could be to ask a Nebraska grand jury to indict a Nebraska lynch mob, even if I could get anyone to name anyone to me.''

Pronto Cross smiled boyishly and said, ''Oh, I don't know. I'd be willing to make an educated guess that the lard you just shot was the leader of the Minute Men the other night.''

Longarm sipped some suds as Doc Forbes looked uncomfortable. Cat-and-mouse games seldom paid off unless you had at least a few face cards to flash, and he knew that they knew that he knew, so what the hell.

Longarm took another swig, but put the schooner down for good half full. Like most old soldiers, Longarm could go seventy-two hours without sleep as long as things stayed interesting. But he was starting to feel the effects of no sleep and a heap of Nancy Calder as they talked in circles. So he said, ''I have to get my livery mount back to its stall and some well-deserved rest. I'll see you after dinner at that hearing, Doc, and by the way, could I have a carbon copy of all the testimony from the hearing on that Sunday school teacher?''

Doc Forbes looked surprised, but said, ''I can rustle you up an extra carbon. But what use might you have for it? Mildred Powell was murdered by Howard Bubblehead Burnside at a time your federal want had an ironclad alibi. He was in jail, waiting for you to come pick him up, when the sheriff arrested that Mongolian idiot out at his sister's hog farm. Dancing Dave was simply swept up in the generally festive mood when the Minute Men came for Bubblehead, see?''

Longarm said, ''I'd see better if I had it all on paper to go over all at once. It would save me asking questions such as how far out of town that imbecile boy had to walk or run from First Calvinist, or who had proper jurisdiction over a crime committed in town by a kid with a more rural address.''

Pronto Cross started to repeat what he'd said about the township and county having a gentleman's agreement. Longarm cut him off and said they'd talk about it later, after he'd had some sleep and read some testimony. Then he left before either the town or county could get around to arresting him.

As he dismounted out front of the red livery, he saw everyone was up early at the Widow MacUlric's boardinghouse next door. He led the jaded chestnut inside and tipped the sleepy night hostler a dime to make sure his pal got a rubdown and fresh water in his trough for a tolerable ride with no shying or balking.

As he walked next door a female voice chirped like a bird, and then the more mature Widow MacUlric was off her porch and running to greet him, gasping, "Oh, Custis, we've been so worried about you! A maniac with a ten-gauge shotgun just tried to murder you in your sleep and where on earth have you been all this time?"

He answered in a calmer tone, "Hunting maniacs. They told me over to Main Street about the excitement here. Needless to say, I wasn't where they expected to find me at that hour."

The smaller Ellen Brent from the library came down the steps to join them as she chirped, "We thought you were dead at first. They made a dreadful mess of your poor bed and left the air filled with a blizzard of goosedown! You say it was more than one? Do you have any idea who'd do such a dreadful thing, Custis?"

Longarm nodded soberly and said, "The late Porky Shaw seems to have been at least involved. He announced my demise prematurely and panicked when he saw me still alive. We figure there was somebody with him who packed a shotgun."

Mavis MacUlric declared, "That's for certain! Thank God you were somewhere else when all that number-nine buck tore up through the floor and your mattress! We're going to have to put you in that back room I first suggested until I

76

can see about some new bedding and repairs.''

He started to ask where that might leave *her* sleeping. He decided it was up to the lady of the house to say in front of the others. Two of the men who boarded there were out on the porch now. Before Longarm could ask where that Preston cuss from the *Advertiser* might be, with or without a Greener, the skinny cuss joined the others up yonder in his bathrobe.

Longarm followed the two gals up the steps. One of the men near the front door said, ''Welcome home and see what you just missed!''

Longarm strode into the front vestibule as another boarder raised a candlestick to show him the well-perforated pressed-tin ceiling. You could still smell the gunsmoke. Longarm nodded and said, ''Ten or twelve pistol rounds and two shotgun blasts for certain. Have you ever had the feeling someone you'd never done anything to just didn't like you?''

As he led a sort of promenade up the stairs, the printer from the *Advertiser* volunteered, ''Everyone in town heard you'd made it plain that Pawnee Junction wasn't big enough for you and Porky Shaw. Isn't it obvious he didn't want to leave?''

Longarm swung around the newel at the second-story landing as he replied in a disgusted tone, ''Talking like that is talking like kids after school. He tried to back me down at the barbershop. I didn't want to. I told him I was at his service. I never told him he had to leave town.''

As he led the way into his hired front room and struck a match to light the wall lamp, another male boarder opined, ''Somebody else must have told him a man with two guns and a big mouth was supposed to fish or cut bait. Nobody in living memory ever stood up to that bully and made him eat crow. He must have thought we all expected him to clean your plow if he ever wanted to back anyone else down.''

Longarm didn't argue as he lit the lamp and took in the mess a fusillade of small-arms fire had made of his hired room.

The feather down had settled to the oiled planking all around the bedstead. The rumpled bedding looked as though more than one poor bird had been stood before a firing squad and then dragged off by the heels, still flapping. The ceiling above, papered a plain yellow, had been peppered and torn considerably. At least one slug had ripped up one wall to lay open the floral paper and expose the torn underlayer of railroad and Confederate bonds. Turning to the landlady in the doorway, Longarm said, "I'm sure sorry about this, Miss Mavis. Before you argue, I want you to listen tight. It was an agent of the U.S. Government they were aiming at, and like I said, I get to charge valid expenses to the same. So I'm fixing to have all this damage repaired for you at government expense."

She said, "Well, I suppose I've no choice about the mattress. I just can't afford a new one and that one's done for. But there's no need to get fancy up here, seeing it's not a room I usually let out to anyone."

He said, "I thought I just told you not to argue. Whether you hire the room out or sleep in it your ownself, it was shot up because of me and I mean to put things right by you."

He glanced out the window. The summer day was already dawning in the east, but it was still sort of early. So he added, "I aim to lie down and catch a few winks before breakfast because I might have another long day ahead of me. So if it's all the same with you folks . . ."

Mavis MacUlric protested, "You can't lie down on that ripped-open bedding. I'm up for the day. Why don't you just nap in the room I've been using and we'll wake you when your breakfast is ready."

He started to argue, failed to come up with a sensible reason to refuse her kind offer, and in no time at all was stretched out on top of her quilt counterpane in his duds and socks, knocked for a loop by darkness behind a locked door and the clean floral smell of a friendly gal's Florida water and the lilac sachets she'd tucked under a fresh pillow for him.

Sparky little Ellen Brent came to wake him in what felt like less than five minutes. But he was feeling more wide awake by the time the two gals had him eating buttermilk waffles downstairs. The other men who boarded there had eaten up and lit out for work by then. So he knew they'd let him lie slugabed as long as they'd dared.

Longarm didn't want to mention his intended visit to the hardware store before he had to. So he allowed he had to see about any night letters at the Western Union, and offered to walk Ellen over to her job at the town library. For some reason that got the Widow MacUlric to dropping cups on her floor again as they lit out together.

Longarm didn't say anything as he helped the library gal down the steps. Ellen sighed and said, ''I hope she doesn't think I'm trying to steal you away from her.''

''Were you fixing to start your own boardinghouse, Miss Ellen?'' Longarm asked in an innocent tone.

The perky brunette giggled and said, ''Don't play shy schoolboy with me, you wicked thing. We've all heard what a Don Juan you've been with those faster girls of Denver!''

To which he could only reply, ''You have my word I haven't been fast with a single slower gal from Pawnee Junction.'' Which was true, as soon as one studied on where Nurse Calder had been from.

Ellen said, ''Don't hurt her, Custis. I know she's attractive and Lord knows she's vulnerable. But she was very happy with the one true love of her life, and the only man who's sparked her since was a brute who was only after her property.''

Talking about other brutes was more comfortable than defending his own weak nature. So along the way he brought her up to date on some of his cleaner recent adventures, and absorbed the sad story of an almost rich widow who'd been about to sign over her heavily mortgaged house to a slick-talking boarder when he'd suddenly had to leave town, one jump ahead of the bounty hunters hired by a far richer gal he'd swindled.

Ellen said, "It seems he'd get lonely widows to sign over their all for him to manage, just before or after they got married. Needless to say, he sold everything they'd signed over and lit out with the cash, whether they were properly wed or not."

Longarm said he'd heard there were skunks like that. Then he helped her open and air the library, and left the two books he'd borrowed where they belonged in the stacks before he said he'd see her at their boardinghouse later. He didn't say he'd come by after the inquest later in the day because he wasn't sure whether he'd be spending another night in Pawnee Junction or not.

As he was walking down toward the Western Union by the railroad stop, one of the townsmen from the saloon earlier fell in beside him to say, "Fox Bancroft is in town. Along with a dozen riders off the Diamond B. Thought you'd care to hear."

Longarm nodded soberly and replied, "I thank you for your words of cheer. They told me Porky Shaw was the boss wrangler out to the Diamond B. I take it this Fox Bancroft is the ramrod?"

His informant shook his head. "Owner. In town to attend the hearing and decide whether you or old Porky was in the wrong, to hear Fox declare it."

Longarm grimaced and muttered, "I sure wish folks wouldn't declare such things. They tend to paint themselves into a corner no matter how things turn out, and they never sent me here on any fool fox hunt!"

Chapter 11

Billy Vail's night letter, wired cheap when the telegraph traffic got slack in the wee small hours, said old Billy was mighty chagrined about Dancing Dave doing that rope dance before he could sing. Then he opined a federal investigation of local vigilante activity could get as tedious as bailing brine against a rising tide unless the local law was willing to level with outsiders.

Longarm wired back the reasons why he had to attend that coroner's hearing after dinner, and added he'd try for the evening southbound if his investigation seemed ended with the death of Porky Shaw. He felt his boss would settle for a leader of the lynch mob shot fair and square. Billy Vail's notions of justice were Old Testament. He only demanded an eye for an eye and a tooth for a tooth, and since Dancing Dave had been a disgusting cuss in his own right, old Porky Shaw's fat dead ass likely balanced the scales of that blindfolded statue in Judge Dickerson's courtroom.

Longarm walked north from the Western Union to the sprawling lumberyard and hardware outlet of the informative Remington Ramsay, who turned out to be a blond giant in his forties with his stomach still flat from hefting nail kegs and two-by-fours around. Old Ramsay got even friendlier when Longarm said he'd read that book about the Ramsay family intermarrying with all those interesting folks before they got around to founding Pawnee Junction.

The hardware mogul bragged less than his privately printed book, and graciously allowed that the U.S. Army, the railroad, and the first herds up to greener grazing had helped him some.

Longarm said he was in the market for a nice sheet of pressed ceiling tin, a couple of rolls of wallpaper—plain yellow, and in that same floral pattern, if they had it—along with some finishing nails, wallpaper paste, and such.

Ramsay nodded, but asked if Longarm had the tools he'd need to use all that stuff, adding, "You ought to make sure you have some paint for the ceiling metal too. Sounds like you've cut yourself a big slice of redecorating. Not that it's any of my business."

Longarm said, "It ain't no secret. I've been boarding with that Widow MacUlric, and last night somebody shot her place up trying to get at me. I figure the least I can do is put things back the way I found 'em when I first moved in."

Ramsay said he'd heard the gunplay the night before, and congratulated Longarm on his brush with Porky Shaw, saying, "Somebody was sure to shoot such a pain in the ass, and I'm glad it was a lawman from other parts. We have enough steam simmering around here without a blood feud over a tub of lard."

Longarm cocked a brow and asked, "Do tell? From your book I just read I'd gained the impression all the white folks in these part were just one big happy family."

Ramsay shrugged and said, "I wrote that brief history over a year ago. Why don't I run over to that boardinghouse with you and have a look at what needs to be done before I sell you the wrong stuff to do it with? I'm a general contractor as well as a merchant and, I hope you won't take this wrong, it's often cheaper in the long run to pay a professional than to do it yourself."

Longarm started to say he'd always been handy enough with tools and simple repairs. Then he wondered why he'd want to say anything like that when he had a local historian gassing away at him like the hostess of a church social.

Longarm allowed he valued the opinion of a professional hardware man and house fixer. So Ramsay called one of his lumberyard helpers over to say he'd be out for a while and to just sell stuff but not sign any papers on his own.

Longarm was afoot that morning. But Ramsay had his buckboard hitched up out back. So they rode the short distance in style, if one found Missouri mules stylish.

They found the Widow MacUlric alone with her broom and dust mop at mid-morning. It turned out she and the hardware man knew one another on a business basis. He'd sold her that orange-flower wallpaper way back when, and allowed he could order the same pattern for her if she was dead set on it. He agreed with Longarm that it would be easier to replace the bullet-riddled ceiling tin than attempt to make it look like new. As she led them upstairs, Mavis MacUlric asked how long it would take Ramsay to get her the same pattern she and her late Martin had picked out in their golden yesterday when it had still looked as if they'd chosen the best location in town.

Ramsay said, "I remember the two of you starting out to pioneer as purveyors of room and board, Miss Mavis. Mr. MacUlric was a man who kept his word and paid his bills on time. Might you be of Scotch descent as well?"

She brushed a strand of hair from her brow and replied, "*He* was. My people were Pennsylvania Dutch. What has that to do with wallpaper?"

The man who sold the stuff by the gross said, "They keep changing the pattern. Some ladies seem to admire new wallpaper patterns as the time to paper over draws nigh. I'm sure I can get you this particular pattern if you'll give me time to write back and forth to more than one wholesale supplier I do business with. On the other hand, I have stock on hand right now that should give the same general effect.''

She stared wistfully at the ugly bullet gouge through her familiar orange, spinach, and mustard pattern. Longarm was about to suggest the same colors with a different design, or a similar design with different colors, might not be too bad, when the beefy blond hardware man stepped over to the wall and knelt to run thoughtful fingers along the torn edges, assuring her as if she was a little kid whose heart had been set on a particular play-pretty, ''I suppose we *could* fill it in and smooth it over, then watercolor over to hide the gap.''

''Oh, could you?'' the young widow gasped hopefully. Then she beat Longarm to the punch by asking, ''Wouldn't hiring such an artist cost an awful lot?''

Ramsay smiled like an older boy showing little kids how to bait a hook as he modestly replied, ''I've always been handy with a paintbrush, ma'am. It's not as if you need the services of a Rembrandt or even Currier and Ives here. It should be easy to match and feather in the background color. Then it's just a matter of daubing orange and green edges where they really look torn away. It should only take me a few hours, giving the background wash time to dry before I fake in the rest. I'd naturally feel silly charging anyone for just fooling around like that.''

She protested there was no way on earth she'd ever let anyone go to that much trouble for nothing.

Longarm said, ''He's making a modest profit on the materials. Ain't that right, Mr. Ramsay?''

The helpful hardware man rose back to his considerable height as he gravely replied, ''I am. Let's consider my helping with the repairs part of the deal. Who knows, I might end up with a whole new line as a wallpaper repair man as word gets around and night riders keep shooting at Deputy Long here.''

The three of them laughed. Longarm was starting to like

the cuss in spite of his dumb book about family trees. Long-arm asked, "What about the floor, ceiling paper, and such?"

Ramsay raised the new bedding and mattress from one corner of the bedsprings to see daylight lancing up through the floorboards, and said, "Driving in pegs, planing them flat, and staining them to match ought to serve where nobody's liable to look too closely to begin with. That ceiling paper's a mite smoke-stained as well as plain. So it makes more sense to just paper over."

Longarm pointed at the one wall papered with old Confederate and railroad bonds, asking what Ramsay thought they ought to do about that.

The hardware man shrugged and said, "I assumed that engraved bond paper held some sentimental value. Would you like us to paper that wall with some pattern that might harmonize, Miss Mavis?"

She hesitated, shook her head, and decided, "Fair is fair and that was the way I'd hired this room out to Custis here. I'm not being sentimental. You can see, where it's torn, that I papered over a lot more of those worthless stocks and bonds before we got to the last roll up here in this one front room. But maybe some other time, after I've fixed things around here that really need fixing."

Then she said, "I have to get down to my kitchen and see about a roast I put in just before the two of you arrived. You'll be staying for dinner out back with us, won't you, Mr. Ramsay?"

Ramsay looked surprised, but said he'd be delighted.

Longarm was neither that surprised nor delighted. He'd only set out to fix up her house, not fix her up with a cuss who bragged on all the fancy folks he claimed as kin. Sometimes it seemed as if Lexington and Concord had been a waste of gunpowder to some self-styled fine old American families. For it seemed they'd no sooner gotten shed of that stuck-up English peerage than they'd taken to sprouting coats of arms and claiming descent from kings, queens, and other mythical beings.

Longarm was surprised at the tone of his own voice when he allowed he had other chores that morning and might as well get cracking, seeing that the handsome hardware man seemed to want to tether his mules in the shade and help her set the table.

Longarm caught himself stomping as he strode away, and had to laugh at his own natural but foolish feelings. He paused on the cinder path to light a cheroot before moving on in restored humor.

The last thing a man who might be leaving on the evening train had any use for had to be a lonely widow in the market for a strong man to lean on. From the little he really knew about Remington Ramsay, old Mavis was likely as well off leaning on him as any other skirt-chasing son of a bitch in town. The husky bastard was surely fixing to prong her, and somehow Longarm knew she'd take her pronging sweet and submissive, at least compared to that clinical Nancy Calder. But a man had to be a sport about the ones he just couldn't have, and there was just no way any man could plan on having them all, dad blast it.

So he ambled on over to Doc Forbes to find the doc had gone out on a call but left those carbon copies for Longarm in care of his wife—who wanted to coffee and cake Longarm as well.

Longarm thanked her for the invitation, but said he had other pressing chores. So she let him go, and he went over to the smaller saloon a few doors up from the Red Rooster to order a beer, carry it over to a corner table, and sip suds on his own as he went over the testimony taken down at the inquest that had started all this bullshit.

Longarm had been told more than once about those two cowhands hearing screams from the cellar of First Calvinist as they were on their way into town. Neither claimed to have seen Bubblehead Burnside do it, or even run past them. They just told the same pathetic tale of a pretty gal lying there with her skirts up around her hips and blood all around. Rafe Jennings was the one who claimed she'd told him "Howard" had done her so dirty. Nick Olsen had been riding hard for help as the poor gal gurgled her last in Rafe's arms.

Longarm lit a thoughtful cheroot as he muttered, "So that's just one man's word as to the words of a dying woman."

Then he got down to the testimony of Timmy Sears, aged seven and hence just within the limits of lawful testimony, who'd been crossing the churchyard on the far side as the two cowhands reined in. Timmy allowed a "big boy called Howard" had dashed out a cellar door on his side of the building when he'd heard Miss Mildred crying real loud.

Longarm wouldn't have questioned the kid any closer than one of the members of the panel had, once Timmy was asked if he meant he'd seen that half-wit Howard they called Bubblehead. Timmy's exact words were: "Miss Mildred told us not to call Howard Bubblehead. She said it wasn't his fault he looked like that."

Longarm blew a thoughtful smoke ring and muttered, "It seems the missionaries most anxious to help wind up in the pot. Folks who won't associate with anyone out of the ordinary hardly ever have anything extraordinary happen to them."

He sipped some suds and told the carbon papers spread out in front of him, "All right, despite what Dr. Langdon Down and others say about kids like Bubblehead Burnside being gentle-natured and innocent of horny notions, a dying woman's accusations work better than some diabolical plot involving two cowhands who didn't attend her church and a Sunday school kid who did. Those syndrome studies say that there's no sharp line betwixt them and the rest of us. Some look more Mongol than others. Some are drooling idiots, whilst others may be smart enough to leave home and support themselves. So who's to say some ain't as innocent as babies about sex whilst others might at least wonder what those hogs, dogs, and bigger kids are up to? Doc Forbes allows in this autopsy report that it didn't seem as if the Sunday school teacher had been thoroughly raped. He never said nobody could have tried!''

By now it was getting on toward dinnertime, and Miss Mavis had said something about a roast in the oven. But Longarm saw they'd just laid out a tolerable free lunch at one end of the bar. So he decided to stay put and read over the damned carbons until he saw what he was missing.

On the face of things, he wasn't missing anything. It was far easier to believe Timmy Sears had seen Howard Burnside fleeing from the scene of the crime than it was to picture a seven-year-old boy as a murder-rapist, with a cowhand who hadn't raped anybody seriously lying to cover up for the kid. But damn it, Bubblehead Burnside had been playing in the dirt like an even younger kid when the posse had ridden out to his sister's hog farm.

Longarm got up to go pay for another beer and help himself to a salami on rye and some boiled eggs as he muttered, ''Sure. Bubblehead Burnside was a fiendishly cunning criminal who was only pretending to be a Mongoloid idiot so that nobody would suspect him of being a sex maniac. The way they decided at the hearing was the most sensible way it works and that's that, dad blast it!''

Then he carried his beer and free lunch back to the table to go over it all some more, dad blast it.

Chapter 12

The inquest that afternoon was just a formality, and would have been over sooner if it hadn't been for Longarm. Doc Forbes congratulated him on his marksmanship, and the county prosecutor, who turned out to be that older cuss in the stylish white deerskin jacket and Buffalo Bill face hair, declared there was no call to present a fair fight the loser had started before the circuit court, even if it *had* been in session.

Everyone seemed satisfied except Longarm, who got to his feet when the coroner asked if there were any objections to quitting while they were ahead.

Longarm said, "I've been going over the transcript of that earlier inquest, Doc, and no offense, that young Timmy Sears was questioned once over lightly when you consider how serious his testimony was."

There came a confused murmur from the panel, and their audience as well. Doc Forbes asked, "What in thunder might Timmy Sears know about the late Porky Shaw slapping leather on a federal lawman with a rep? The child was fast asleep on the far side of town at the time!"

Longarm nodded, but pointed out, "He was crossing the churchyard the day Mildred Powell was assaulted and murdered. On the face of it, his few recorded words back the tales told by the grown men who say they found her lying in a pool of blood and accusing that retarded boy. But I'd feel better if I could have a few words with young Timmy as well.''

The county prosecutor snapped, "Thunderation and Sweet Jesus, the case of the People versus Howard Burnside is moot! Whether Bubblehead done the deed or not, the Minute Men strung him up. So what else might there be to say about it?''

"Who done it if Howard Burnside didn't,'' Longarm replied in a voice of calm reason. "That's the trouble with lynching folks before they can stand trial. I agree it looks as if that retarded boy made a play for his Sunday school teacher, stabbed her when she told him not to be silly, and ran out the cellar door the way Timmy Sears seems to say he did. I still want to talk to Timmy Sears.''

The town law, Pronto Cross, called out from the back, "It's almost supper time. What say I rustle young Timmy and his folks up in the morning and have them over to my office for you to interview around nine or ten?''

Longarm allowed that sounded fair. The county prosecutor gussied up like a cavalry scout said he'd be switched with snakes if Longarm could show him anything they'd done wrong the last time they'd questioned the kid.

Longarm said, "I just said I'd read over every word you all took down. The first time you read over it he seems to be certain a boy he knew as Howard because you weren't supposed to call him Bubblehead came out of that church cellar about the time Timmy heard Miss Mildred screaming for help. But when you read it over more than once . . . Let's just say I'd like to go over it one more time with the boy, hear?''

Pronto Cross said they had a deal, and Doc Forbes declared his inquest into the death of Porky Shaw closed. So all rose to get on home or over to the Red Rooster before supper time.

As he was waiting for the crowd to clear, a mighty handsome gal brushed past him wearing her red hair in braids under a black Spanish hat, with a Schofield .45 in a tooled leather holster on either seam of her whipcord riding skirt. He couldn't tell if she noticed him or not. No man could have. Gals who carried their noses that high in the sky could pass between a train wreck and a Roman orgy without letting on they noticed either.

Longarm turned down an invitation to supper from Doc Forbes, and told the county prosecutor and town marshal he might see them over at the Red Rooster later. So they left together without pestering him further. He was about to leave when one of those gents he'd seen the other day in the barbershop sidled up to him to say, "Before you cloud up and rain all over me, Deputy Long, I am only passing on a message from a cuss who said he was in too much of a hurry to talk to you personal."

Longarm cocked a brow and dryly replied, "I've had such messages relayed to me in the past. They do that more often down Mexico way. Who sent you, the Minute Men or this Fox Bancroft I've heard so much about?"

The cuss from the barbershop said, "I don't recall. I'm only trying to be helpful. I was told to tell you there's a southbound combination passing through this evening. That gives you time to have supper, settle up with anyone you owe here in Pawnee Junction, and be safely on your way by sundown."

Longarm asked, "What happens if I'm still here after sundown?"

The townsman looked sincerely worried and asked. "Who's to say? I ain't armed and I ain't threatening anybody with shit. I've only told you what I was told to tell you, see?"

Longarm nodded thoughtfully. If he shoved this worried-looking older cuss against the wall and shoved a .44-40 muzzle up one nostril, he might or might not get a true name or more out of him. But after that, as they'd long since noticed down Mexico way, it could be a waste of time trying to follow a tangled thread from one mere lickspittle to another, and worse yet, that was sometimes exactly what they expected you to do. He'd walked into a swell ambush in Sonora one night trying to find out who'd sent Pancho to tell Juanito to tell Hernando. So he contented himself with: "Tell your pals I'll take their railroad timetable under advisement."

Then he lit a smoke out front, and circled the courthouse to duck between two buildings and sneak over to the library and catch little Ellen Brent just as she was fixing to close for the afternoon.

She let him back inside when he allowed he'd like her to. As she shut the front door after them she said, "We missed you at dinner. That hardware tycoon, Remington Ramsay, took your place under the grape arbor and ate enough for the both of you. What are we going to do about him, Custis?"

Longarm smiled uncertainly and replied, "Didn't know we had any call to do anything about him, Miss Ellen. I asked him to come over and give me an estimate on the damage from that gunplay in the wee small hours."

Ellen shot the bolt of the door as she said, "I fear you may have created a monster. He was still there when I had to get back to work and leave poor Mavis to his mercy!"

Longarm said, "I noticed he seemed sort of smitten with a still young and handsome widow woman."

"Her property, you mean!" sniffed the snippy brunette. "I know he was flirting with her a lot, but all the time he was going on about losing his own spouse to the ague a good spell back, he was eyeing everything inside her picket fence as if he already owned it. I told you about that other skunk who came courting a poor woman with little experience with smooth talk, didn't I?"

Longarm said, "You did. She's lucky to have a more

wordly well-read librarian as a chaperone. I can see a man would have to get up early to put anything over on you. Do you have any books about that old Credit Mobilier of America scandal as broke during the '72 Presidential race?''

She said she thought there might be something on it in the recent history cross-index, and led him over to her files as she confessed she'd heard about them doing something dreadful with railroad stock back in Washington while she was in high school in Omaha. She confessed she'd been more interested in a certain boy down the street at the time.

As she pored through her index cards Longarm said, ''I was just getting over my admiration for cows at the time. They were still at it about Credit Mobilier when I signed on with the Justice Department as a junior deputy. But they never asked my opinion, and I'm not certain I recall the skullduggery right.''

She sighed and said, ''I don't have anything filed under Credit or Mobilier. If we have anything about the mess it would be in a book we have under another listing. Maybe if you could just get me started with the gist of it all . . .''

Longarm sighed and said, ''I fear everyone wound up mighty confused with all the facts and figures laid out in front of them. The way I remember it, some big railroading men got authorized by Congress to build that transcontinental railroad betwixt '64 and '69, under mighty generous terms. The government was so anxious to see a railroad all the way out to California that they loaned both the Union Pacific and Central Pacific millions of dollars and granted them alternate sections of land all along their rights of way, along with the water, timber, and mineral rights.''

She said, ''I heard about that. I wish somebody would give me just one square mile of free land, with or without a forest or gold mine on it!''

Longarm nodded. ''The hard-nosed directors of that Central Pacific were content with just getting as rich as King Midas. But a couple of *Union* Pacific directors called Ames and Durant took pork-swilling to new heights. They set up a dummy corporation, called the Credit Mobilier of America, to contract with the Union Pacific the two of them already ran to lay the tracks out to the Great Salt Lake and pound gold spikes with the eastbound Central Pacific.''

"Was that against the law?'' She asked.

Longarm said, ''They're still arguing about that. The exact numbers are in those books you don't have handy. But the left hand billed the right hand a third more than it really cost for every mile of track. Ames and Durant, as Union Pacific directors, were proud to pay Ames and Durant of Credit Mobilier such a handsome profit with other suckers' money. Oakes Ames sat in Congress as well as on all those boards of directors. So he figured he'd best cut some politicos their own slices of the pie. He dealt out shares in Credit Mobilier cut-rate or even on credit, which could be considered outright bribery, and was by some. For as those golden spikes got driven and the construction company was liquidated, Credit Mobilier shares with a face value of around two hundred dollars were redeemed with cash and Union Pacific paper worth over eight hundred dollars per share, which does add up when you slip a congressman a few hundred free shares at a time. That may have been why so few came forward.''

She said, ''I'm not sure I understand what those congressmen were supposed to *do* for all that railroad paper, Custis.''

Longarm said, ''Neither was that congressional panel after they'd looked under many a shell. They never found out how many shares, worth what, were distributed amid how many congressmen to do what. They managed to implicate Vice President Colfax, two senators, and four or five representatives, along with old Ames himself. But nobody was ever indicted or even expelled. The committee likely missed a few old boys holding handsome blocks of Credit Mobilier. In the end the dummy outfit that built the Union Pacific faded away like that Cheshire cat in the story about Miss Alice in Wonderland, leaving more of a bad taste in the air than any big grin.''

Ellen asked, ''Aren't those Credit Mobilier certificates under all that wallpaper back at the house worth anything at all?''

Longarm said, ''That's how come I want to look 'em up. I'm only a lawman, not a stockbroker. I don't *think* they could be worth anything at this late date. Martin MacUlric couldn't have thought much of them when he used them to paper his upstairs before he passed on. But he did buy a heap of them before he decided they were only pretty paper.''

Ellen said, ''I never met him. But if you ask me he must have been a fool. Why would he have paid anything for all that Confederate money?''

Longarm shook his head and replied, ''Not money. Bonds. A promise on the part of the Confederate States of America to pay the bearer face value on maturity. He wasn't a *total* fool. Some of the former states of the Confederacy *have* started to pay pensions to Confederate widows, now that the Reconstruction has blown over and Southerners are running Southern states again.''

Ellen gasped. ''Good heavens, she has ever so many Confederate bonds back at our boardinghouse!''

He chuckled and said, ''There's no way even the *Union* could afford to redeem all that rebel paper. They had to issue a heap of it to get any real money in return. But it *might* be possible to redeem old Credit Mobilier of America stock. The parent company, the Union Pacific, is still in business and doing grand under new management. If we can't find anything here, I can wire this railroading slicker I know. Old Jay Gould ain't connected with Union Pacific, but he'd know if any railroad paper was worth a plugged nickel, and I did him a favor one time.''

She said she'd noticed even mean-tempered folks tended to remember favors. That gave him the opening to say, ''Us mean folks don't get as many favors as some. I came here with the intention of asking for one. You got me all side-tracked, worried about slick-talking hardware men and upstairs rooms papered with stocks and bonds.''

Ellen said she was only worried about a poor young widow, and asked him what she might be able to do for *him*. She could sure smile dirty for such a big-eyed little thing.

He said, ''I don't want to catch the evening southbound. I don't want to have anyone shooting up our boardinghouse again either. So I have a plan. But I need a little help. I ain't asking anyone to risk hide or property on my account, you understand. I only want to scout around the railroad stop to see if I can spot anybody acting sneaky when the southbound combination steams in and out. Then, if I can't catch any sneaks laying for me near the tracks, I mean to see who's most surprised I'm still in town after the train rolls on without me.''

She smiled up at him like a fond teacher warning the class clown not to write like that on the blackboard, and asked what he wanted *her* to do come sundown.

He said, ''I want you safely hunkered in your quarters at the boardinghouse before my time on the streets of Pawnee Junction runs out. I just said I didn't aim to risk anyone else's hide. But if I could borrow a key to this library, and have your permission to hide out here later on, I'd be in position to catch a few safe winks and mayhaps surprise some villains come morning. I'd have never proven Porky Shaw was a Minute Man if I hadn't shown up bright-eyed and bushy-tailed where he never expected to see me.''

The bookish brunette laughed like a mean little kid and said, ''I have an extra key at home. Is there anything you want me to sneak back from the house after supper?''

He started to say no. Then he had to admit some bedding might be nice. Ellen laughed again and took him by one hand, saying, ''Come with me, you sneaky thing!''

He didn't think it would be polite to tell a pretty gal he just didn't have time to come with her. So he let her lead him through the stacks to what looked like the door to a broom closet.

But when she opened it he saw a flight of stairs leading down to a cellar he hadn't considered. He followed her down, and she struck a match to reveal a vast space of crates and loosely stacked books by the foot of the stairs. Further in, a space had been carved out for a lamp table and an army cot, made up with female notions of bedding.

Pointing at the frilly pillows and patchwork quilt as her match went out, Ellen said, "I use this private nest for reading and relaxation when things are slow. Just don't go upstairs when anyone knocks on the front door and they'll never guess you're down here, see?"

He laughed and said, "I was wondering where you were the first time I came by. This here's a swell hideout, Miss Ellen. But can we have more light on the subject to get out of here now?"

She asked him what the hurry was. She seemed to be standing closer of a sudden. He wanted to grab her so bad he could taste it. But he told her, "I'd rather stay. But I have to get over to the water tower and hide out on top of it before anyone else might expect me to. If I let them get there ahead of me, it might not matter whether I wanted to board that train or not."

Chapter 13

Like most such installations on the western plains, the water tower at Pawnee Junction was fed by its own sunflower windmill pump. The steel maintenance ladder ran skyward between the timber platforms of the windmill and water tower. Longarm glanced casually around to make sure nobody was taking pictures of him, and then he climbed slow and sure, as if he had every good reason in the world to up and have him a look at whatever.

Grab-rails led from the top of the ladder across the slanted roof of the tower to where a sort of trash-can lid covered the inspection manhole at the peak. Longarm crawled up to it, asshole puckered just a mite, and took off his hat so his head would be just a dot against the darkening sky to anybody likely to closely examine a landmark they were used to passing.

He had a grand view in all directions as the sun sank lower in the west, gilding the grassy crests of the rolling swells all around the dinky town. He noticed the town had grown some since Remington Ramsay had mapped it for his local history, but Longarm had to allow the sort of stuck-up hardware man had mapped the place tolerably well. He could make out the courthouse square and municipal corral where Ramsay had drawn them on paper. So that pinpoint of light yonder was coming from that front room he'd hired at the MacUlric house. Old Ramsay would be needing early lamplight if he'd already started on those repairs, and with any luck, the sneaks who'd scouted the boardinghouse for Porky Shaw and that other cuss would report that there was somebody else up yonder this evening. The barnlike county courthouse was shut down for the night. The windows of the library a block away were naturally as dark. Longarm grinned as he thought about that hidey-hole in the library cellar. Then he heard somebody coming loudly along the tracks from behind him, and craned his head to peer over his own shoulder at an awkward angle.

But it turned out to be just a couple of colored boys in their teens, teasing and laughing as they tried to move along the rails like tightrope walkers. One of them was carrying a fishing pole. They'd likely gone looking for catfish up in that impoundment to the north of town.

The colored boys stopped right under Longarm. He was hoping they only needed to take a piss. Then one called out, "I dares you to climb up to the top of that old windmill in the dark, Nero."

Longarm wanted to shake old Nero's hand when he heard another voice reply in a lofty tone, "I *been* to the top of that old tower. They ain't nothing up there worth the climb and we is already late for supper, you fool."

So they walked on, sparing both themselves and Longarm any unpleasant surprises. There didn't seem to be anyone else around, once they were out of sight amid the tin-roofed shanties over on the east side of the tracks. Longarm hadn't noticed any colored folks in Pawnee Junction before. That was doubtless why they were quartered on the far side of the tracks. The boys' folks likely worked for the railroad.

A tedious time later the sun was setting, turning the spire of the nearby First Calvinist Church to a black accusing finger edged in gold as bats commenced to swarm out of it like bees. He had a clear view of the wagon trace those two cowhands would have been following down the far side. The wide yard little Timmy Sears would have been crossing lay between the church, a weed-grown vacant lot, and the tracks. He'd ask the boy when he talked to him what he'd been doing around the railroad stop. From up here on its water tower, there didn't seem to be anything much to tempt small boys.

Then, staring down at the open platform and empty cattle pens in the gathering dusk, Longarm sighed and said, "You're getting old if you can't remember laying double-head nails and pennies on railroad tracks, old son. Don't you remember how the train wheels squashed you all them bitty swords and shields you'd need for your army of really little folks—if you could ever manage to capture and domesticate them?"

The red and purple sky was pretty, and lamps were lighting windows all over town in a way that made a traveling man feel left out and wistful. Longarm didn't know why he ought to feel wistful about all those settled couples, happy or otherwise, who'd had their suppers and might soon be going to bed to do all sorts of things, naughty and nice. For while it was true he had to be missing out on one hell of a lot of naughty and nice, he'd *still* never get at half the loving down yonder no matter which particular bedroom lamp he got to trim.

Some few stars were coming out as bats fluttered past, some lower than his prone form. One star near the northern horizon seem to be getting bigger. Longarm figured before he heard the distant wail of its steam whistle that the southbound evening combination was coming in on time. Train whistles were another thing that made a body feel wistful when the day was done. Folks all over town would be heaving sighs as that evening train sang its siren song to them in passing. Men fixing to bed down with gals a passing stranger

100

could only dream about in passing would be wishing they could follow that lonesome whistle through the night to someplace like Paris, Camelot, or maybe Kansas City. Human beings were like that. There'd be no need for any man to pack a badge or gun if human beings could make up their fool minds what they *wanted* and be *satisfied* with it. But on the other hand, how many clipper ships or railroad engines had ever been invented by trees, or even sheep?

The train chugged ever closer, and now some few dim figures were moving about down yonder in the gathering dusk. Then the headlight of the slowing locomotive lanced ahead of it down the tracks to shine on nobody more sinister than a fat man with a mail sack and a half-dozen casual-looking men and boys who seemed to admire trains.

The water tower stood north of the loading platform and cattle pens so the engines could water best as they were headed north, up the slight but persistant rise of the Sand-Hill Country. Longarm was just as glad when the engine passed under him, blowing smoke in his face, to hiss to a halt further down, with the passenger cars of the freight-passenger combination right under him. Anybody interested in others getting off or getting on would have to be watching from damn close. But Longarm couldn't spot a lick of suspicious movement as nobody got off or on. Then, farther along the platform, they'd finished swapping mail sacks and loading some freight from Pawnee Junction aboard. Nobody seemed to be expecting any deliveries from anywhere else on the sea of grass that lay all the way north to the Peace River. Then the bell was clanging and the combination was rolling on toward the bright lights of Ogallala again, calling back its haunting song of adventure and romance as it chugged away.

Longarm stayed put. He'd learned as a kid, at a place they called Shiloh, how dumb it could be to move first after things commenced to seem safe. But after he'd counted to a thousand Mississippis, it was really dark and the bats all around were starting to flutter past with the contempt bred of familiarity. So he put his hat back on and slowly made his way down to where you just had to crunch a tad on the railroad ballast if you wanted to get anywhere else.

Nobody else was crunching as he eased his way off railroad property to cross that weed-grown lot and the brooding silence of the churchyard behind First Calvinist. It was easy to picture someone popping out of that dark frame mass as he crossed the churchyard. Timmy Sears hadn't been scared as he might have been because he'd known the one who'd popped. Those mounted cowhands on the far side would have seen the cuss if he'd run any direction but . . . yonder, towards the railroad yards Timmy had just come from.

Longarm got out to the sandy street and headed for the more wide-awake parts of town.

Most of the shops were closed by now. Some ponies were tethered out front of a hole-in-the-wall describing itself as the Aces and Eights Card House. As he eased along the plank walk, he could see over the tops of the painted lower panes of the front windows. If anyone inside cared, he saw nobody staring back at him. That snooty redhead he'd seen at the coroner's inquest was seated at a table between the bar and swinging doors with some gents dressed cow and a man in a planter's hat and a linen suit. Places regulated as tightly as the Parthenon in Denver or the Long Branch in Dodge never would have allowed a woman to sit in at cards in the main taproom. But Pawnee Junction was a far from tightly regulated town.

Longarm strode on to the larger and more familiar Red Rooster. He left his six-gun holstered, but had his derringer palmed as he stepped through the swinging doors. But nobody seemed to care. He saw some new faces along with many who'd been there when Porky Shaw had slapped leather on him. There was no sign of Porky on the swamped and sawdusted floor that evening.

Longarm saw the buckskinned county prosecutor sitting at

a corner table with another redhead, this one dressed more like a rich widow than a cowgal and owing her hair coloring more to the henna shrubs of the Old World than that other gal seemed to.

Longarm knew how he'd feel if some other gent came over uninvited as he was jawing with a plain or fancy gal. So he moved over to the bar, eased along it to where he had the door, front glass, and most everything else covered, and ordered a scuttle of tap, leaving that palmed derringer right where it felt best, down at his side.

He'd just been served when that same brassy saloon gal came over to ask him what made him think he was better than poor Kiowa Jack.

He gravely replied, "You have the advantage of me, ma'am. I'd have to know who Kiowa Jack was afore I could tell you whether or not I was better than him."

She laughed, turned to the older imitation of Buffalo Bill, and called out, "Says he never heard of you, Kiowa Jack!"

When he saw they were talking about the county prosecutor, Longarm covered up by calling, "I thought you said your name was John."

The man who also seemed to be Kiowa Jack waved the two of them to join him. So they did, with the gal seeming surprised when Longarm held her bentwood chair for her. She turned out to be the Baroness du Prix for some reason. The reasons anyone would call his fool self Kiowa Jack were more mysterious. Buffalo Bill had a rival showman describing himself as Pawnee Bill because he'd once scouted for the army with some Pawnee friendlies. It sounded reasonable to say you were a blood brother to the Pawnee because, like their distant kin, the Cherokee and Mohawk, Pawnee saw things more like white folks than most Indians. That was likely why Cherokee and Mohawk had had so much trouble with white neighbors back East. The less-famous Pawnee went in for more farming around settled villages than their Cheyenne and Arapaho enemies too. So it was easier to make friends with Pawnee as long as you remembered not to walk through their cornfields or mess with their women. But *Kiowa* were contrary next to Comanche or Lakota, and a white man who intimated he was all that close to Kiowa was a born liar or one hell of a diplomat.

Longarm didn't want to hear bullshit about Texas Indians from a Nebraska lawyer with a possible drinking problem and a mighty wild taste in summer dress for certain. So he said he'd just been up by the scene of Mildred Powell's murder. Kiowa Jack sighed and said, "A poor innocent girl who died too soon at the hands of an idiot she was only trying to help. I'll drink to that."

The Baroness du Prix raised her own beer, but sniffed, "Or so they say. I hear she was sort of flirty, for all her Sweet Jesus ways."

"Don't speak ill of the dead," said Kiowa Jack, the county prosecutor, gravely. "I know for a fact you used to be Baptist, and that Sunday school teacher would hardly spend much time over *here.* So there's no way you could have known that much about the lady."

The Baroness du Prix was likely drunker than she let on. Because she snorted, "Oh, I know all about such ladies!" and commenced to sing, "Christ, the savior, I'm his lamb! Jesus Christ! How glad I am!"

Kiowa Jack fixed her sternly with one brow up and the other scowling as he snapped, "That will be enough of that if you don't want to do time on the county roads serving water and pussy to the chain gang, you mean-mouthing slut!"

The Baroness du Prix rose grandly to point in Kiowa Jack's general direction and announce, "Look who's talking, after he begged last night for some French mouthing because he was too drunk to do it right!"

Then she swept out of the taproom before Kiowa Jack could draw on her or send her to jail.

The cow-town lawyer stared sheepishy at Longarm and

softly told him, "She really knows how to French. But I just hate it when a gal talks dirty, don't you?"

Longarm said, "That's likely why they discourage gals and Indians from drinking hard liquor. Was there anything to what she just said about that murdered Sunday school gal?"

Kiowa Jack shook his head and replied, "If only she *had* been. She was pretty and nicely built, but she wouldn't go for a buggy ride if a man proposed marriage ahead of time. Nobody but a jealous old whore or a feeble-minded sex maniac would have taken her friendly nature for flirting. But why are you still droning on about a case we've closed the books on, old son?"

Longarm said, "I ain't closed the books on it yet. Somebody told me earlier I ought to get out of town or consider the effects my staying here might have on a cattle king called Fox Bancroft. Might there be anything you could add to that, Kiowa Jack?"

The older man seemed sincerely puzzled as he replied, "Fox Bancroft is more a cattle *queen* than a cattle *king*. I heard she was in town with some Diamond B riders. Never heard she was after anybody. Heard she was playing cards up the street a piece as a matter of fact."

Longarm blinked and asked, "At the Aces and Eights? A tall redhead, dressed mannish and packing her Schofields side-draw?"

Kiowa Jack nodded to say, "That's our Fox Bancroft, right as rain. You want an introduction to the pretty little thing, old son?"

Longarm rose grimly to his feet, saying, "I reckon I'll just mosey up the street a piece and introduce myself."

Chapter 14

Nobody looked up from the table as Longarm entered the Aces and Eights a few minutes later. He moved over to the bar and ordered a schooner to nurse. As he was served the barkeep murmured, "We don't want any trouble here, Uncle Sam."

Longarm didn't answer as he turned from the change he left on the mock mahogany to study the game with casual interest. If the barkeep knew he was a federal rider, everyone in the place knew he was a federal rider. Moreover, the gal had been sitting near Longarm all through the hearing into his shoot-out with her boss wrangler.

At first you couldn't tell from where he lounged against the bar with his beer in his left hand and a fistful of derringer down at his side. But on second sight, under crueler coal-oil light, the redheaded owner of the Diamond B seemed closer to thirty than sweet sixteen. But she was still worth looking at, despite some sun and wind she'd been through in her time. They called features like hers "classic" when they were carved in marble instead of tanned flesh. The people at the table were playing a sucker game called slapjack, as if *black*jack couldn't clean you out soon enough. He idly wondered whether she was playing slapjack because she was in a hurry to clean everyone else out or just stupid.

Slapjack was a simple game that relied more on eye and hand coordination than luck, when it was played fair.

Once the regular deck had been shuffled and cut, it was dealt out so all the players, in this case four, had his or her own big pile of cards face down. They'd already played some of this particular hand. So everybody had the same dozen or less left. They were playing with house chips. As the deal rotated around the table, each anted yet another chip before one card was moved out to the center of the table by its holder, face down, and then snapped face up by the one whose turn it was. He or she wasn't supposed to do anything but get out of the damned way. If the card was anything but a jack or joker, *nobody* was supposed to do anything and the next player got to deal one card. But if it *was* a jack or joker, the first player other than the dealer who placed a hand flat on it or "slapped Jack" won the pot.

It was all too easy to slap slow, or to mistake a king or a queen for a jack and slap when you weren't supposed to. Anyone slapping a wrong card got to ante double as the action continued. Longarm had to join in the gentle laughter when a young and excited-looking cowhand yelled "Slap Jack" and grabbed for the queen of hearts.

Longarm couldn't tell who was cheating yet. He hadn't been there when the first cards were dealt with a one-way deck. But from the way they kept winning, Longarm would have been willing to bet on either the redhead wearing the black Spanish hat or the fatherly old cuss in the linen suit. The youngest cowhand lost twice more, looking far from happy about it, before the old cuss in crumpled white linen said there was only the joker to be slapped and suggested they start a new round.

Everyone but the chronic loser agreed. The steamed kid got up from the table with a remark about never betting the money he kept in his sock. Longarm drifted casually over to ask the man in white linen if any number could play.

The obvious professional glanced around at his fellow players. Nobody there seemed to want to bite Longarm on the leg. So the man gathering up the cards said, "Buy some dollar chips at the bar and sit down, Deputy Long. They call me Deacon Knox. I'll introduce you to these other sports once we see if you're a serious cardplayer or not."

Longarm moved over to where the barkeep was already stacking white chips on the bar for him. Dollar ante seemed serious indeed for such a kid game in such a dinky establishment. Longarm would have been more worried about his own future if it hadn't been for that one-way deck.

He bought twenty dollars worth of chips and returned to the table without his beer, asking if it was permitted to smoke there. Deacon Knox glanced at Fox Bancroft, who just shrugged. The gambler nodded at Longarm and told him to sit down, asking, "Would you like to shuffle, seeing you just got here and I swear you're not my long-lost child?"

Longarm smiled thinly and said, "Next time, after I light up and settle down here."

So Deacon Knox handed the deck to Fox Bancroft, who shuffled them carefully, though with no flash, while Deacon introduced Longarm to her and the surviving cowhand, called Curly for obvious reasons. After she'd shuffled four times she let Longarm cut, making no comment as he did so awkwardly, thanks to the derringer in his other hand and the unlit cheroot gripped in his grin. Deacon Knox suggested Curly deal. The cowhand did so, awkwardly but carefully, counting out the number of face-down cards he tossed in front of everyone at the small table. Longarm saw right off he was holding two good cards. Curly had dealt himself none, Deacon another pair, and the redhead one.

They all anted up and Curly turned over a ten of clubs, to which nobody responded, and then it was Longarm's turn. He wasn't ready to deal a good card yet. So he turned over a trey of diamonds and that was that. When the deal went to

Fox Bancroft, she turned over the king of clubs and smiled thinly when Curly slapped it and lost.

Longarm wasn't surprised when it was Deacon's turn and the card the old pro turned over was neither of the winners he had to know he was holding. Longarm knew Deacon was letting the pot grow before he raked it in. They both knew Curly wasn't about to turn over a jack or the joker. Then it was Longarm's turn again, and he wasn't about to spoil the fun. So he turned over a four of spades and tried not to look pleased when Fox Bancroft dealt a five of hearts.

They anted some more, and Curly passed the deal on to Longarm with a queen of spades nobody slapped because Curly couldn't and the redhead didn't because she caught herself just in time. Old Deacon, of course, had known all along it wouldn't be a jack or the joker.

Then it was Longarm's turn again, and he decided Fox Bancroft ought to quit while she was ahead. So he moved the card nobody else but old Deacon could read to the center of the table, flipped it over, and snatched back his hand lest the tensed redhead slap him as well as the jack he'd just dealt her.

As she raked in the considerable pot with a more girlish expression than he'd ever noticed on her pretty face before, old Deacon was staring at him thoughtfully. Longarm didn't want to tell the slicker how he'd been slickered. So he just blew a smoke ring across the table at him.

They could all agree there were three jacks and that joker left to play, with the odds of one turning up better, or so Deacon wanted the other suckers in the game to assume.

Longarm didn't argue. He still had one winning card at his disposal. He wasn't sure what he'd wind up with if they dealt fresh again. Deacon had two left. The gal, like Longarm, had one. But if she dealt it, she'd be unable to slap it. So Longarm went along with the Deacon until the pot was getting scary again before he dealt Fox Bancroft another good card to slap before the old pro could come unstuck.

As the redhead gathered her second pot in a row, Longarm suggested they reshuffle and start fresh. Deacon smiled as if he was running for public office and said, "There's still two jacks and a joker somewhere on the table, friend."

Longarm tried to sound friendly as he calmly replied, "I know. You have two slappers and Miss Fox has one. But neither Curly nor me have spit. So how's about being a sport and starting over?"

Deacon Knox got sort of pale, but didn't stop smiling as he asked in a sober tone, "Are you saying you can read the backs of these cards, friend?"

Longarm smiled back at him and said, "Can't you?" Then he turned to the goggle-eyed Fox Bancroft, her eyes staring at him jade-green, to say, "If you'll allow me, ma'am, I'll be proud to pick out the jack or joker you have in front of you."

She stared down frozen as he turned over a jack. Deacon Knox laughed lightly and said, "Lucky guess," as he started to restack the cards in front of *him*. Then he was staring down the muzzle of a Schofield .45 in a work-hardened female hand as Fox Bancroft quietly asked Longarm to put up or shut up.

Longarm reached across the table to turn over the remaining jack and joker as he stared past the ashen Deacon to warn the barkeep, "I thought you said you didn't want any trouble in here."

The barkeep straightened up and put both palms flat on the bar in front of him as Fox Bancroft stared soberly at Deacon and quietly purred, "You've been playing us false all this time with a marked deck, you poor dead son of a bitch."

Longarm said, "I wish you wouldn't kill him, ma'am. Fair is fair and he wasn't suckering you with a marked deck. What happened was partly your own fault, and how's he supposed to pay back all he won off you if you blow out his brains and wind up in jail?"

She flashed her jade eyes at Longarm, snapping, "Nobody is about to put this child in jail for shooting skunks out of season. What do you mean it was partly my fault? I wasn't the one dealing marked cards and . . . Say, come to think of it, those are *my* cards! I wasn't born yesterday, so I bought a fresh sealed deck off that barkeep and . . ."

Then she was on her feet, six-gun trained on the barkeep as she called out loud enough to mill a stampede, "How did you *do* that, God damn your eyes? I asked for a sealed deck and you said you were *selling* me a sealed deck, brand-new, you dirty card-marking rascal!"

Longarm leaned back in his seat, took a drag on his smoke, and calmly said, "It *was* a fresh sealed deck and nobody marked a single card, Miss Fox. Simmer down and I'll explain whilst Deacon and yonder barkeep fetch all you paid for all the chips you lost from the till. You *were* fixing to do that, weren't you, Deacon?"

The man in white linen rose with a gallant defeated smile to say he'd been about to suggest that very thing. The imperious armed and dangerous redhead sat back down beside Longarm, saying, "This had better be good."

Longarm picked up two cards and placed them face down in front of her, saying, "This one's a face card and this other one ain't. I looked at them before I put them face down, of course. Can't you see the different way the backs of the two cards read?"

She stared down hard and said, "No. They both have the same dumb flowers stuck in that same flowerpot. Am I missing something in the small lines of the black and white engraving?"

He said, "Nope. The bland line drawings on the backs of the cards are identical, printed from the same plates to show that same vase of flowers no matter what's on the other side. Don't you see it yet? Do you brand your fool calves on both sides, or upside down?"

She sniffed, "Don't be silly, we naturally brand every calf

111

on the near side and . . . Oh, Good Lord, I feel so stupid!''

"Well, you ought to," said Longarm, not unkindly, as he explained, "Cards ain't like calves. It doesn't show when you turn a jack upside down because each jack has two heads. When professional gamblers buy fresh decks they buy cards with the *backs* as well as the *fronts* reversible. This brand, stocked by a place advertising itself as a serious card house, was never meant for anything more serious than kids playing for matches. Ladies who play whist at purely social gatherings have been known to read these so-called one-way cards. Old Deacon never had to mark them. He just had to make sure the jacks and joker alone were turned the opposite way from all the others in the deck. After that, he could tell in advance whether he was fixing to slap at a card or not. I thought it might be fun to pick out a slapper from my pile, reverse it some *more*, and give you a chance to beat him to the slap when we both caught him napping. I noticed he never tensed up to slap when he didn't think there was a jack or joker fixing to be turned over.''

She laughed and said, "They were right about you."

Deacon Knox came back to the table with a big stack of bills. He gravely placed them in front of her and said, "This is all the money Matt took in from the bunch of you this evening. I sure hope we can settle this misunderstanding quietly."

She said, "It's up to the *Advertiser* and *Monitor* whether they want to print my confession of stupidity or not." Then she called, "Hey, Slats, get over here and let me give you back your money, you pouty thing!"

Then, as Longarm sat there smoking, Fox Bancroft divided the pile of wilted bills with as much skill and likely more honesty than your average banker might have managed.

As she did so, Deacon Knox was heard to plead, "Don't put us out of business, Miss Fox! Your education ain't cost you a thing, and where does it say you have to educate the rest of this wicked world?"

She coldly replied, "The Good Book. Thou shalt not steal or play with one-way decks. I just added that commandment because I doubt old Moses had anyone as sneaky as this lawman advising him about gents like you. I sure wish he'd been here the *last* time we rode in, you son of a bitch!"

Deacon said, "I want to make it up to you, pretty lady. So I'll tell you what I'm going to do!"

But Fox Bancroft said, "*I'll* tell you what you're going to do. You're going to get out of town. That's all you *can* do for anyone as pretty and rich as I am. I'm giving you to the end of this month to find a buyer for this place and—"

"But I don't own this place!" the tinhorn shouted as the barkeep wailed, "Neither do I! We're working for Mr. Remington Ramsay, the owner of this whole business block!"

Fox Bancroft said, "Good! I'll settle with that hardware monger later. There's a northbound combination coming through tomorrow morn. Be on it when it leaves and we'll say no more about it."

Deacon Knox protested, "I have no call to travel north, pretty lady. As a matter of fact, I have some old enemies up that way and I'd as soon head for Ogallala and the U.P. Line if it's all the same with you."

The hard-eyed redhead rose to her full five-foot-six as she blazed, "It's not all the same with me. I've given you cheating bastards more than enough time to pack you ill-gotten gains. By noon tomorrow I may not be the only one in these parts with a bone to pick with you. Would you rather take your chances with old enemies who may not have any call to expect you, or would you rather be here in Pawnee Junction when the Minute Men get word of your transgressions?"

Deacon said he was just leaving, and the worried-looking cuss on the far side of the bar said the last round of drinks would be on him if they didn't mind his closing early.

As Longarm rose to stride over to the bar with Fox and all the others, she fixed her jade-green eyes on him to quietly ask when *he* might be leaving Pawnee Junction.

He locked eyes with her to say as calmly, "Hard to say. I figured on leaving when I was ready. Are you saying I ain't welcome around your fair city, Miss Fox?"

The redhead leaned casually against the bar, replying, "It ain't my fair city. I only own and operate the Diamond B and that's enough to keep me busy, most of the time. To answer your question about the way I feel about you shooting my boss wrangler, I was at the inquest and I never told anyone to shoot up any boardinghouses or slap leather on a lawman with a rep."

She suddenly smiled up at him, as if the sun had suddenly appeared in a cloudy sky, and added, "I can't say I was feeling all that friendly towards you until you took my part and saved me so much money just now. It only cost me seventy-five dollars to have Porky buried in a nice box in ground I had to spare. So we're more than even and you've nothing to fear from me or mine."

Longarm said he wasn't at feud with the Diamond B either. Then he tried, "Might you be in position to speak for those Minute Men, ma'am?"

The hard question didn't shake her. Her voice was just as firm when she replied, "I have never run a brand or ridden anywhere with a sack over my head."

He insisted, "That's not what I asked, Miss Fox."

She said, "I know what you're asking. What my hired help, friends, and neighbors do on their own time is up to them. So when they hear how many of them might have been cheated by this bunch, there's just no telling what they might decide to do about it. I'm in no position to give orders to anybody I don't have on my payroll."

"How many Minute Men do you have on your payroll?" he just couldn't help from asking.

Fox Bancroft smiled right back at him and said, "I just said you and me were square. I never said I wanted to sell any kith or kin to the law. I told you it ain't up to this girl whether they ride or not. So why don't you take my advice in the spirit I sincerely mean it and get out of town before it's too late?''

Chapter 15

Longarm lit the small lamp by the narrow cot in the cellar of the officially vacant library, and stacked his gun rig and hat atop stacked books before he sat down to light a cheroot and haul off his boots.

It had been a mighty long day, and he wasn't looking forward to one as tedious. Common sense and likely Billy Vail were telling him there was nothing keeping him in Pawnee Junction. It seemed doubtful there'd be any damned conviction if he *did* discover more about the Minute Men. He'd have one hell of a time getting any member of that mob to testify truthfully against any pals who might still be alive. Folks who refused to name any members of the mob were already marketing the late Porky Shaw as the leader who'd done all the actual killing. What Billy Vail had said about trying to get the goods on a popular local gang had been all too true. Frank and Jesse were still at large, after all this time, because whole counties of Missouri folks just wouldn't talk about who they might or might not have seen in church the Sunday last.

Gripping the cheroot in his teeth, Longarm undressed and got under the sheet and one thin quilt. But he stayed propped on one elbow as he smoked the cheroot down. He didn't want to get too comfortable while he smoked in bed. He knew he shouldn't be smoking at all. But he just wasn't tired enough to let go all the way. He spied some books Ellen Brent had set atop the table for her own reclining reading. Longarm reached out and discovered one was a tract by Miss Virginia Woodhull, the exponent of women's rights to vote and screw around just like men.

The other was an English translation of that Hindu Kama Sutra on the art of screwing. Illustrated. He'd thought little Ellen had seemed sort of flushed and out of breath when she'd taken so long to answer the door that time.

Longarm had read the same publication before. But he naturally thumbed through it to look at the pictures, being a man of normal manly tastes. He smiled fondly as he recalled poring over the Kama Sutra down Mexico way with a pal of the female persuasion who was game to try anything. They'd made dead certain that some of the illustrated positions were just plain impossible, although others had sure been fun.

He knew it would be even tougher to go to sleep if he hit the two pillows with an empty stomach and a hard-on. So he put the dirty books back where he'd found them, snuffed the smoke, and trimmed the lamp. He lay there a million years, staring up at the darkness as his stomach growled. He was otherwise sleepy as hell, and he didn't know where he'd be able to order a meal in such a small town this late at night. He cursed himself for not thinking about that earlier. Like most men of action, he tended to forget about eating and sleeping when he was up and about. So this wouldn't be the first time he'd toss and turn a bit before he ever got to sleep.

So he was still wide awake a spell later when he heard somebody walking across the library floor above him. It sounded like somebody trying to walk soft, in high-heeled boots.

Longarm slowly sat up to silently grope in the darkness

for his .44-40 as, sure enough, those sneaky footsteps faded toward the rear of the main room above. Then he heard the cellar door's latch click, and so he thumbed the hammer of his six-gun back. The side arm fired double-action with a good hard yank on the trigger, of course, but the trigger was hair-set if you cocked the hammer first, and a man sitting naked in a dark cellar with somebody creaking down the stairs at him just never knew how much time he'd have to work with.

Then a match flared and Longarm almost fired at the sudden glow before Ellen Brent called out, "Hello, Custis, are you there?"

Longarm eased the hammer back down as he called back, "Been here some time, ma'am. I'm in bed without no duds on, before you come any closer."

She followed her flickering match flame around a high stack of books anyway, saying, "I brought you some sandwiches and a canister of lemon punch from the house, seeing you missed supper with us. We have to talk about poor Mavis and that sneaky hardware man!"

She shook out her burnt-down match, struck another, and sat down to perch her little round bottom on the rail of his cot as she struck another and lit the table lamp, adding, "I thought he'd never leave this evening! That's why I'm so late. I couldn't leave poor Mavis at the mercy of that Romeo!"

Longarm put his six-gun away, and reclined on that same elbow as he saw she'd indeed brought a picnic hamper along with her. As she began to pile food and refreshment atop the little table, Longarm asked her with one eyebrow raised, "What were you so worried about? Aside from those grown men boarding there, well within range of a good scream, a widow woman is by definition a lady of some experience with horny men."

The unwed brunette said knowingly, "Remington Ramsay is too smooth to make a clumsy grab at poor unworldly Ma-

vis. I know what he's up to. They were up there poking and
fussing at the walls and woodwork until he had her giggling
like a schoolgirl. He means to take his own sweet time on all
that repairing and redecorating, and then he means to come at
her with flowers, candy, and a proposal of marriage!''

Longarm laughed out loud and asked, ''You figure that's
a dirty way to treat a lady?''

To which she replied, offering him a ham-on-rye sandwich, ''It is when that's not what you're really after! I told
you I was keeping an eye, and an ear, on them. I heard him
telling her he could repaper all of your room and the front
hall cheap if she'd settle for new paper in some other design.
He invited her right out to come over to his hardware store
and go through all the pattern books he had to show off. But
that was only the half of it! He got to picking at loose wallpaper hither and yon, like it was scabby, and then he marveled out loud that Mavis and her poor dead Martin had
started out with all the upstairs walls done in old stocks and
bonds.''

As she poured lemon punch in tumblers for the two of
them Longarm said, ''*I* commented on it when I saw all those
pictures of Confederate officials and railroad engines. To tell
the truth I'd worry more about a man without glasses pretending they weren't there at all. Say, this is sure a swell
ham sandwich, ma'am!''

She handed him his drink saying, ''Thank you. I made it
myself, in the dark, speaking of sneaks. I didn't think you'd
want me telling anyone where you were. Mavis asked if I
knew where you were when you didn't come back after that
oily hardware monger left. Can't you see he's after her property, like that other wretch who trifled with her affections?''

Longarm washed down some ham and rye with the lemon
punch she must have mixed in the dark as well. He grinned
and said, ''Lord love you, you put just the right amount of
lemon juice in this rum, Miss Ellen. As to Remington Ramsay, aside from his bragging book, I now know for a fact

119

that he already owns considerable property here in Pawnee Junction and he never had to marry up with anyone he didn't like to get it. As a dealer in lumber and hardware who got in on the ground floor, he was naturally set to buy building sites and build on them cheap, for sale or rental. He must be rich enough by now. I haven't had time to find out what those Credit Mobilier bonds and stock certificates are worth. I told you I'd try. How much time do you figure we have before the minister calls out for us to speak now or forever hold our peace?''

She didn't smile back. She said, ''This is serious, Custis. Mavis must be more hard-up than I thought. She barely knew Remington Ramsay, as a tradesman, and now he has her blushing and gushing as if they were already courting. You mark my word, he'll be in her bed long before any minister has anything to say about it!''

Then she gasped, blushed darkly in the lamplight, and looked flustered. ''Oh, I shouldn't have spoken so boldly to a man! Whatever must you think of me?''

He said soothingly, ''That's all right. I've read what Miss Virginia Woodhull has to say about honesty betwixt the genders, and she makes a lot of sense. Albeit I ain't sure I go along with her on women smoking in public. Not cigars leastways.''

The perky librarian had just taken a sip of the mighty strong lemon punch—she didn't seem hungry—when her big sloe eyes took in books she'd left on the table. Longarm had replaced them on the far side of the lamp. The library girl gasped, ''Good heavens, what are those books doing there?''

To which Longarm could only reply, ''Somebody must have put them there. I know I never did. But to tell the truth, I've read them both before.''

She giggled and said, ''You ought to be ashamed of yourself! Or does everyone in a big city such as Denver practice free love in the Oriental manner?''

He washed down the last of his first sandwich and reached

for a second as he delicately replied, "Not *all* the folks in Denver, ma'am, just the high-toned folks on Capitol Hill and the lowlifes down on the flood plain of the South Platte. I read somewhere how prosperous middle-class folks worry more about Queen Victoria's notions of prim and proper behavior than Queen Victoria seems to. Neither the folks with no education nor the folks with a *heap* of education seem to worry as much about such matters."

She poured herself more refreshment as she confided, wide-eyed, how she'd read the same thing, asking in a breathless tone if Longarm thought those rumors about the Widow of Windsor and her burly Scotch butler, Mr. Brown, were true.

Longarm washed down some grub and replied with a shrug that he was in no position to say, adding, "I hardly ever get invited to Windsor Castle, and when I do stay over Her Majesty never invites me into her bedchamber. I figure it's up to the lady and anyone she *might* invite to say what goes on behind closed doors."

Ellen stared thoughtfully at him in the soft light of her secret nest as she mused, "I guess there's no harm if no harm's done. Do you think that's what those sophisticated high-society folks have to say about the wild and wicked things they do?"

He said, "Ain't sure it's wicked if you're smart enough to temper your wildness with sensible precautions. Dumb trashy folks wind up in all sorts of trouble, with no moral code, because it's *dumb* to just do anything you want, with anybody, at any time. Ain't no way a man can get drunk and trifle with his baby sister in a public place without somebody calling the law. On the other hand, as long as Queen Victoria and that brawny Scot wait until they're all alone, and lock the door, there's just no saying what they may or may not be getting away with."

She sighed and said, "It seems unfair to the rest of us.

Why are us middle-class girls denied all the fun of either discreet or foolish fun?''

Longarm told her cautiously, "It's likely on account of the middle-class men you hang around with. There's a heap to be said for middle-class morality. It keeps life simple and nobody looks foolish if they just behave all the time as if somebody was watching."

She finished her drink, started to pour another, then reached for the lamp's trimmer as she demurely asked if Longarm thought anyone was watching.

He replied just as innocently, "Why don't we put out that lamp so nobody could see what we're up to in any case?"

So then the cellar was plunged in ink-black darkness and Ellen was all over him in the dark, with nothing on under that thin summer dress she'd left the house in. So in less time than it took her to say she couldn't understand what had gotten into her, he'd gotten into her and she seemed to want more, despite her small size, in every way, as he pounded her good on that firm army cot.

It sure seemed a caution how women could be so different without having to be ugly. The petite brunette's smaller but plumper body was not only a swell contrast, but her approach to enjoying the mutual pleasure was nothing like the forceful screwing of Nurse Nancy Calder, bless them both.

Bubbly little Ellen was one of those rare women blessed with a healthy appetite and uncomplicated plumbing. For all her reading of illustrated instruction books, she just liked a fair-size man on top and in her deep, with no cares in the world about tricky angles or difficult chords on her old banjo.

They came close together, the way lovers in romantic tragedies were supposed to. Then they got her sweetly rounded rump on a pillow and he felt sure, as he posted in the old love saddle with her soft thighs around his waist, that he'd never in this world find another gal whose whole body seemed so tailor-made to pleasure his. So when she moaned and begged him to leave it in her forever and never.take it out, he found it easy to promise her he wouldn't.

A man had to watch himself around gals like Ellen Brent. For they were tempting as hell, but naturally, nobody who screwed so swell the first night could avoid giving in quickly to the temptation all of womankind suffered. For reasons only someone like Professor Darwin might savvy, they all felt honor-bound to change a man for the better as soon as they had him wrapped around their fingers, and Ellen Brent was about as wrapping a gal as he'd met up with lately.

Chapter 16

Since Ellen was easy to satisfy as well as warm-natured, Longarm wound up with a good night's sleep for a change. The free-thinking librarian didn't want anyone wondering where she was come breakfast time at the boardinghouse, so she got dressed to sneak back there just as Longarm was beginning to notice how crowded an army cot was unless you were both in the middle.

Once she'd locked the front door upstairs behind her, Longarm lay back with a satisfied sigh, and slept like a log until he heard her now-familiar heels overhead again. She'd opened the library just a tad early after breakfast at the boardinghouse to serve Longarm his own breakfast in bed. He'd have never known it was that long after sunrise if he hadn't had hot buttered toast, black coffee, and some more of *her* to wake himself up in that windowless dark cellar.

Once she had him up, in every way, Ellen said she had to open the library officially. So he let her, taking his own time to put on his clothes and mosey upstairs after her. A couple of schoolgals who were jawing with Ellen at her desk looked surprised as all get-out to see a tall stranger wearing a gun appear out of nowhere. So Longarm nodded casually at Ellen, declared, "I put that travel book about India back where it belongs, ma'am," and sauntered on out the front door as if he was leaving church on the Sabbath.

First things coming first, he went back to the boarding-house to clean up and change to a fresh shirt and underdrawers, just as glad to meet nobody upstairs or down until he was fixing to leave.

He found his messed-up room about as he'd last seen it. But as he went back downstairs and out the back door, the Widow MacUlric and old Remington Ramsay drove up the side lane on that two-mule buckboard. Mavis MacUlric had on a summer-weight Sunday dress and sunbonnet. The hardware man was wearing bib overalls and a denim work shirt. The wagon bed behind them was lightly laden with nail kegs, bags and buckets of paint, and Lord only knows what-all.

Mavis MacUlric said, "Oh, there you are, Custis. We missed you at breakfast and I was so afraid you'd come home to find you quarters in disarray. Remington here just sold me on a whole new wallpaper pattern, and I may let him redecorate the whole house!"

Longarm locked eyes with the hardware mogul, who seemed to read minds, because he softly said, "On me. As I was just explaining to Miss Mavis, we in the interior-decorating trade often do demonstration jobs gratis to convince other customers we know what we are up to. Miss Mavis has agreed to let me conduct tours of just her parlor and hallways once we finish up here."

"Once *we* finish up?" Longarm asked.

"My helpers will be here any minute with a portable steam boiler we use to peel wallpaper," the big galoot replied without looking away.

The pretty young widow woman Ramsay was being so good to dimpled down from the buckboard seat and explained, "Remington says it's best to peel down to the plaster and start all over."

The mighty thorough-sounding redecorator swung down

to hold out a helping hand to the lady as he told Longarm, "Three layers of paper and wheat paste are begging for bugs to begin with. But as a matter of fact, as I just told Miss Mavis, those old railroad stocks and bonds her late husband pasted up as good for nothing might just be worth something."

As he helped her down, the young widow woman said, "Oh, Remington, poor Martin may not have been as practical as *some* men I know, but he was hardly a fool who'd paper our upstairs wall with valuable stocks and bonds."

Ramsay gravely replied, "I never found your late husband anything but sensible when we were talking business, ma'am. At the same time, we'll never have a better chance to steam all that Confederate and Credit Mobilier bond paper off, clean it, dry it, and see just what you've had hidden up yonder all this time. You and your Martin were likely right about it being worthless. But it never hurts to ask, and it's certainly not worth anything, even as wallpaper, hidden under the new patterns you just picked out!"

Longarm said something about having to get on over to the Western Union, and left them to hammer that dumb-sounding dispute out. But even as he walked the short distance to the telegraph office, he wondered whether Remington Ramsay was an easygoing innocent cuss with nothing up his sleeve, or one mighty slick confidence man out to skin a poor widow woman. For it worked either way. Marrying up with a gal sounded like a mighty desperate way to get her valuable wallpaper, while a widow woman who had some of the same would tend to trust a man who came right out and helped her cash in on unsuspected wealth to where he might not *have* to marry up with her to rob her blind.

Striding across the sandy street in the dazzling morning sunlight and noting it was shaping up to be a scorcher, Longarm muttered, "Gals in love with a sweet-talking lover are likely to sign anything, and Ellen says she was nearly taken by such a bastard earlier!''

He caught himself mapping out a plan of action, and warned himself with a cynical laugh, ''Forget it! You'd have never heard about all the woes of a somewhat horny and mighty nice-looking widow woman if you hadn't wound up playing slap and tickle with another gal entirely. Dropping Ellen like a used snot rag to go after Mavis would be mean to the both of them. It ain't as if you were planning on staying in these parts. So even if you *could* save Mavis from that hardware monger for a spell, she'd likely wind up going back to him as soon as your back was turned.''

He entered the cooler telegraph office to find no messages there for him, and sent a slew of his own messages in every direction. Then he said he'd be back, and moseyed up the street to the town marshal's office. He found it far smaller than the sheriff's office and county jail on the far side of the courthouse. Pronto Cross was seated at a desk in the middle of the twenty-by-forty-foot frame building. The one holding cage they had, empty at the moment, shared the back wall with the crapper and rear exit. Save for a few extra chairs and the gun racks along one wall, the effect was spartan, and made the modest space seem bigger than it really was.

Cross got up from the desk and said, ''You just missed Timmy Sears and his mother. She brought him over to talk to you, like I asked last night. Seeing it was so early and you weren't here yet, they said they'd be back in a spell. She said something about shopping, and he was asking if she'd buy him some marbles.''

By tacit agreement the two of them stepped outside to the shaded plank walk so the Sears woman would see Longarm was there as she and her kid dashed all over the tiny town in the hot sun.

Longarm offered the town law a cheroot, and got them both lit up before Cross told him, ''I didn't question the boy again about the time he spied Bubblehead Burnside fleeing the scene of his crime. His folks weren't too happy about the boy having to go over it all again. Tim Sears Senior says little Timmy has been pestering them since the killing about what such words as rape might mean. Seems the other kids have been talking to him about what happened to their Sunday school teacher. But that might be the least of our worries.''

Longarm took a thoughtful drag on his own smoke and said he only had a couple of gentle questions to ask little Timmy. Then he asked what other worries Cross might be talking about.

The town law said, ''Two strangers in town. Got off the morning train and vanished into thin air. Never stopped anywhere to order a meal or hire any horses. So where are they *at*? You know there's no proper hotel here in town, and I have my two roundsmen canvassing everyone with rooms to let.''

Longarm shrugged and said, ''Try her this way. Strangers to *you* might not have been strangers to somebody in town without a sign in their front window. What did these spooky strangers look like?''

Pronto Cross said, ''Spooky strangers. I didn't get too close a look at either. I was standing across from the open platform in the shade when they got off unexpected. I figured they might be with *you*, no offense, because of the dark suits and six-guns carried cross-draw. I had no sensible-sounding reason to dash across the street and introduce myself, so I never did. I figured they'd settle down somewhere, with or without asking about you, and I could approach them more delicate. So I let 'em walk on by, blast my sweet nature, and now I don't know who they were or what they got off here to do!''

Longarm took another thoughtful drag and decided, ''They could be no more than innocent visitors. If they're holed up for the moment with local kith or kin, you'll see them around town sooner or later.''

"What if I don't?" asked the town law. "What if they ain't innocent at all? What if they're here to rob the bank or something?"

Longarm said, "Don't get your bowels in an uproar. Get word to anyone with a horse to hire that you'd sure like to hear about anyone new in town hiring a horse. There's no train in or out of here this side of supper time. Can you see bank robbers escaping afoot across open sand-hill range with enough of a load to matter?"

Cross smiled thinly at the picture and said, "I wish the damned sheriff was handy today. He's rode down to Ogallala, and I can't tell his deputies what to do without his permission. So how am I supposed to stake out the livery, the bank, and Lord knows what-all with just my own two elves?"

Longarm said, "It's getting too hot to put the stew on the stove before you know you'll be serving any, Pronto! All you know for certain is that two gents you don't know got off that train to do, so far, not a solitary thing. It's quiet as hell all up and down the street right now. Matter of fact, I don't see anything going on, and the only living soul in sight would seem to be that tabby cat across the way, licking its fool self in the shade. You say Sheriff Wigan had to go down to the main line at Ogallala?"

Cross nodded, but said, "Don't ask me why. I don't tell him when I go to the card house, and that reminds me. What's this I hear about you telling Deacon Knox to get out of town?"

Longarm answered with a clear conscience, "I advised him it might be good for his health. I caught him dealing slapjack with a one-way deck last night. But I wasn't the one who ordered him to leave town."

Cross said dryly, "I know. They tell me Fox Bancroft was out to shut down the whole shebang. She's always been a willful child. How do you like the owners of the Aces and Eights sending away for some outside help? Deacon Knox is just a two-bit tinhorn, but I happen to know who really owns that joint.''

Longarm said, ''So do I. We were just now discussing wallpaper. I didn't want to discuss more serious business in front of a lady. But since that other lady and her kid seem to be hiding out in some fool ladies' notions or candy store, what else can you tell me about old Remington Ramsay?''

The town law made a wry face and said, ''Aside from the fact that his shit don't stink? He owns half the town. He *says* he only rents out space to the highest bidder and has no personal interest in the whoring and gambling that may go on under roofs he tar-papered personal. I've wired places he says he's done business in in the past. As far as I have been told in return, he's never been charged with anything really serious.''

Longarm soberly asked, ''What's on his yellow sheets that may not sound really serious?''

Pronto Cross shrugged and said, ''Put a man in a Chicago hospital with his fists back in '76. Busted the arm of a blacksmith down in Ogallala just after he came out our way. In both cases the victims are said to have insulted his late wife. You've likely noticed old Ramsay runs to size, and still does a lot of heavy work alongside his hired help. I'd approach him polite if I was going to ask him about the Aces and Eights, pard.''

Longarm shrugged and said, ''Ain't my row to hoe. Up to the township to decide such matters. In the lawful manner, I mean. What have you got here, the usual mayor and board of aldermen handing out business permits for a nominal fee?''

Cross nodded and said that was about the size of it, adding that the county council collected the property taxes. A hot and dusty-looking younger gent was coming their way up the walk now. As he approached he wearily called out, ''You must have seen two pistol-packing ghosts, Boss. I've been all over this fool town and not another soul seems to have seen hide nor hair of your mysterious strangers!''

Pronto Cross said, "Never mind about them for the moment. Deputy Long here has been waiting a spell on Mrs. Sears and her Timmy. Might you have any notion where *they* could be right now?''

The roundsman shook his head and said, "Not hardly. Last time I saw 'em they were here with you.''

Pronto Cross replied, "They went off to buy some ribbon bows or mayhaps some root beers. Try the candy shop down the other way and send Stretch to me if you run across him, will you?''

The already overheated roundsman went off muttering, softly cussing all mothers of small witnesses who couldn't sit still on hot days.

Longarm and the town law smoked their cheroots down twice, and the tall drink of water called Stretch had joined them to say he had no idea where the fool kid and his mother might be either, by the time it commenced to make Longarm uneasy.

He said, "The only sensible place nobody has looked would be the house they live in. The boy or his mother might have taken to feeling poorly in this heat, or just went home for an early noon dinner.''

But it took Pronto Cross less than a quarter hour to establish little Timmy Sears and his mother were neither at home nor at the saddle shop where Tim Sears Senior worked.

The worried father joined the search, which didn't take long in a town as small as Pawnee Junction. But search high or search low, nobody they talked to could say, or *would* say, where in blue blazes the missing mother and son had disappeared to in bright sunlight on what had been described as a short shopping errand.

So Pronto Cross said, "Damn, if only Sheriff Wigan was here, I'd ask him to posse up!''

Longarm said, "You don't have to wait on him. *I'm* here,

131

and as a federal lawman I have the authority to convene a posse comitatus. So why don't we get cracking? It's barely past noon, and how far could anybody carry a small boy and his mother across wide-open range?''

Chapter 17

It took less than an hour to gather better than fifty willing riders and swear them in as a federal posse. Most of them worked or spent a lot of time in town. None of them showed up with masks on. So there was just no saying how many might have assembled for other riding in these parts in the past. Tim Sears Senior himself showed up with a saddle mule and a Spencer .52 carbine. Remington Ramsay had changed his bib overalls for old cavalry pants and rode a handsome cordovan Morgan, armed with a brace of Navy Colts and his Springfield .45-75. A couple of sheriff's deputies as well as both of the town marshal's roundsmen volunteered. Longarm was the one who pointed out that somebody in the law-enforcement trade ought to be watching all the stores as well as their one bank. Pronto Cross laughed sheepishly and allowed he'd forgotten those strangers who'd come in aboard the morning train.

Cross told his own boys they couldn't tag along, and one sheriff's deputy agreed to stay behind and make sure nobody carried off the courthouse in broad daylight, as everyone else rode south along the railroad tracks at first.

They split into two parties at that railroad trestle the Minute Men had used more than once as a handy gallows. Cross led one bunch circling to the west. Longarm and his two dozen riders took the east, and they agreed to meet near that impoundment north of town.

The legal definition of a township extended roughly three miles north, south, east, and west of the city hall on Courthouse Square.

In practice, few cow towns sprawled half that wide when you took in the modest produce, butter, and egg spreads catering to the local market. One of the townsmen riding with him told Longarm they grew mostly garden truck off to the western upwind farms close to town. Longarm didn't ask why they penned more pigs, chickens, and dairy cows over this way downwind. There sure were a lot of small hardscrabble spreads within sight of First Calvinist's white spire. When Longarm commented on that, Remington Ramsay volunteered that filing homestead claims within the limits of a township was not allowed. He said you had to beg, borrow, or steal a plot of ground that big *before* you and your pals incorporated a township on top of it.

Longarm dryly asked if that was how Ramsay had wound up with so much property in town. The big frog of the little puddle sighed and said, "I *wish* I'd got here first. But I thought you read my history of Pawnee Junction. It was carved out of a railroad grant, sold off in one-hundred-by-two-hundred-foot lots at fair prices when they laid out a water stop hereabouts and decided they might as well drum up some freight and passenger business. I confess with a clear conscience that the lots my late wife and me bought cheap are worth way more now."

Longarm muttered, "You said in your book how that great-uncle back in the old country cornered the market in imported lumber. I don't see how anybody could ride through countryside this settled in broad day with an unwilling woman and child, do you?"

Neither the local big frog nor any of the lesser lights

within earshot saw fit to argue. Longarm spied two small snot-nosed kids watching them over some snow fencing alongside the wagon trace they were riding. He swung across the roadside weeds to talk to them rather than yell, the little gal already staring big-eyed and ready to bolt.

He reined in his livery bay at conversational range and asked the kids if they'd seen another little boy and his momma passing by since breakfast. The boy of about six or seven said they just come out to play after their noon dinner.

Longarm had no better luck a furlong up the trace, where an old man with a hoe was regarding them all with interest as he stood shin-deep in cabbage sprouts. When Longarm agreed the big prairie grasshoppers could sure be a bother with garden truck, then asked about a grown woman and small boy being bothered by anybody, the old man in the cabbage patch said he hadn't seen anything more suspicious than these son-of-a-bitching bugs they grew out here in the sand hills. He almost sounded as if he was bragging when he added nobody anywhere had ever suffered plagues of bigger, meaner, hungrier insects. Hence Longarm didn't tell him what they said about Mormon crickets on the far side of the Rockies.

They rode on encountering the same results as they passed by many a spread and questioned many a nester up and about at this busy time of day. Nobody had seen any other strangers in recent memory.

There was nobody in sight as they rode by the hog farm of Rose Burnside. The pens were empty and there was a "For Sale" sign nailed to the door of the flat-roofed sod house. One of Sheriff Wigan's deputies volunteered they'd had no trouble spotting her Mongoloid idiot kid brother at a distance. "He was on his hands and knees this side of yonder soddy, playing marbles in the dirt as if he didn't have a care in the world. When we asked him why he'd been so rough with Mildred Powell, the funny-looking cuss just grinned and said he loved her. Ain't that a bitch?"

"Let's have a look inside," Longarm replied, heeling his mount in that direction. Remington Ramsay started to ask why, then followed, saying, "Right. Miss Rose has been boarding in town whilst she ties up her few loose ends in these parts. So we're talking about an empty house a lot of folks know of as empty!"

But that was all they found when they dismounted to scout all sides through the grimy glass windows. The discouraged Rose Burnside had apparently already sold off the furniture and stove, leaving just an empty shell that somehow looked sort of spooky.

Empty houses all seemed haunted, even when they didn't have any ghost stories attached to them. The human eye was used to reading the sign that others left as they occupied their property. It was likely the *lack* of signs of recent living that made vacant property seem so *unlived* in and hence creepy. Even critters felt uneasy around their own kind lying ominously still and starting to get dusty and musty.

They rode on, asking everyone they met about the missing mother and child. They passed the colored shantytown, built closer to the tracks by the section hands who kept the north-south spur line in repair. One of the old-timers Longarm had seen earlier in that barbershop opined there was just no way any darkies could kidnap a white woman and her boy in the middle of town in broad daylight without anyone noticing. He added, "We only have a few darkies up this way and they seem to know their place. You never see them along Main Street unless they've been sent there on some errand. They have their own general store up the other side of the stockyards. Mrs. Sears would have no call to shop *there,* of course."

Longarm was glad Tim Sears Senior was riding with Pronto Cross. He had to allow his informant seemed as fair-minded about colored folks as a man who called them darkies ever got.

They rode on past a good-sized chicken run, and then they

saw Pronto and the others who'd circled to the west were already waiting up ahead by the low clay dam of that broad pond to the east of the tracks. So they rode on up to join them.

As Longarm reined in near his fellow lawman, Pronto smiled wearily and declared, "Nobody we passed saw a thing. Before you ask, I just asked those colored boys yonder about whether we ought to drag this pond or not."

As Longarm spotted the two kids he'd seen the night before under the shady crowns of some poolside boxelder, Remington Ramsay told them, "Don't have to drag it. I can have my yard hands *drain* it for you any time you like. It's only a yard deep in the middle and you can see that dam is just clay."

Pronto Cross said, "Well, them colored kids say they've been here fishing since before we first missed Timmy and his mother. But seeing it would be so easy . . . What do you think, Longarm?"

The more experienced lawman fished out a smoke and lit it before he said, "I reckon it depends on whose property we're talking about and whether we charge those two young fishermen with criminal conspiracy. What else can you tell us about this overgrown puddle, Ramsay?"

The hardware and construction king of Pawnee Junction made a wry face at the broad expanse of stagnant water. "You've described it about right. The railroad ran that dam across the draw from yonder track bed. They thought they'd wind up with something much grander. I told them what would happen. In the end they had to sink a tube well like the rest of us ignorant peasants. You don't dam surface streams for fun and profit in the Nebraska Sand Hills."

Longarm mildly observed, "No offense, but it seems to me they did so, here at least."

Remington Ramsay snorted in disgust and swept the back of his free hand across the watery view, insisting, "A quarter mile long, a furlong across, and most of it inches deep. All the grassy swells you see around us are stabilized sand dunes, held in place by thick sod, on top of the mud flats of some dried-up inland sea. I dig a lot of cellars and sink a lot of tube wells for others on contract. So I can tell you it's much the same no matter where you dig down in these parts. You dig or drill through a yard or so of sand, it gets moister as you go, till you hit a layer of soggy black muck over clay hardpan. You drill down through the clay into clean reliable groundwater in a swamping bed of coarse wet sand I've yet to drill all the way down through. There's no need to. You can pump it all day and all night without worry, once you're down through that clay. This pond you're looking at lies on *top* of that clay. It's fed by the rainwater soaking down through the sand hills all around, and vice versa. That's why it's never deeper, and can't get any deeper, than the seasonal weather warrants. By late summer you'll see more mud than water north of this dumb dam. I've offered to drain their mistake for them in exchange for the recovered bottomland, but you know how some railroad surveyors are about admitting mistakes.''

Longarm dryly muttered, ''I've noticed you're interested in railroad construction, Ramsay. But I reckon we'd best leave this big mud puddle alone, seeing none of us own it and those kids don't recall anyone being thrown in recently.''

He gazed thoughtfully about, cheroot gripped jauntily in his teeth, then said, ''Well, neither Timmy nor his mother seem anywhere in the vicinity of town. Anyone riding north around the far side of the tracks from this impoundment would follow the rairoad service road. So I reckon that's our best bet.''

Pronto Cross said, ''Speak for yourself, Longarm. I told you before that Sheriff Wigan and me have a gentlemen's agreement about jurisdiction. We're about as far out of town as me and mine usually police.''

Longarm said, ''This situation ain't usual, and we could always tell Sheriff Wigan you were with me.''

But Pronto Cross insisted, "You ride on if you've a mind to. I'm going back to watch the store. I'd risk a tiff with Sheriff Wigan if there seemed the slightest call to. But damn it, there's no evidence that missing woman and her boy were ever this close to the township boundaries, and even if those mysterious strangers *did* ride off with them, who's to say they couldn't have carried them east, west, or to the south just as easy?"

Longarm shrugged and said, "You have to eat an apple one bite at a time. The way north seems less crowded than any of the ways I've seen so far. I'm headed up that way till I come up with a grander notion. I'll see you back in town later, Pronto."

Longarm heeled his mount toward the west end of the clay dam. When Tim Sears Senior fell in beside him, he wasn't surprised. But when he saw Remington Ramsay was still with him, he had to ask, "Ain't we headed in the general direction of the Diamond B and Miss Fox Bancroft, pard?"

The blond giant nodded in a casual way and replied, "Fox grazes her stock west of the tracks for a good many miles. The Rocking Seven owned by Sheriff Wigan's in-laws, the Newtons, ranges as many miles east of the tracks, by one of those gentlemen's agreements Pronto just mentioned. Neither the Bancrofts nor the Newtons actually hold legal title to more than a section or so of home spread. But grazing the sand hills as open range is the only sensible way to raise anything on them in any bulk. I just told you about water in these parts. You can grub a few acres of produce where the bottomlands lie flat and the sand's not too deep. But plow most anywhere else, and the winds will blow your crop away before it can sprout."

Longarm headed around the banks of the broad shallow pond toward those colored kids with fishing poles as he told Ramsay he knew about the geology of the Sand Hill Country and said, "You did hear about Fox Bancroft being at feud

139

with the entire establishment of the Aces and Eights, didn't you?''

Ramsay nodded and replied in an unworried tone, "I own that whole business block. It's not for me to say whether the ribbon bows sold in the notions shop are genuine silk or not. I rent business property to those who care to do business with others on their own. Should you care to open a whore-house or a gambling den, I require three months' rent in advance as security. So I haven't lost any money on an old friend's daughter running those tinhorns out of town. I'll have new tenants in there long before three months have passed.''

Longarm muttered, "One big happy family, unless you ride in from somewhere else, eh?''

Then he reined in near the clump of boxelder as the two youths stood up warily, fishing poles drooping. Longarm smiled down at the one he recognized by name and said, "Howdy, Nero. I reckon that other lawman told you we were looking for a little white boy and his momma, didn't he?''

Nero said, "Sessuh. We never seen he momma but we mind bitty Timmy. He be a nice friendly chile. He play mar-bles good for anybody bitty as him!''

Tim Sears Senior blurted out, "Damn it, if we told Timmy once we told a hundred times not to play over here by the tracks with these . . . ah, other children.''

Longarm hushed him with a warning look and said, "Let's not worry about that right now. I'm trying to find out if these friends of Timmy can help us find him.''

Nero chimed in with the innocence of ignorance and a clear conscience. "Oh, me and Calvin here ain't that bitty white boy's friends. They let us play too. But they mostly plays together along the tracks. Bitty Timmy and that bigger white boy he call Howard.''

The kid called Calvin volunteered, "That big boy, How-ard, he be *mean*. Scare my baby sister half to death, shaking his pink dick at her!''

140

Chapter 18

So Longarm wondered, even as he was riding on, why he was riding on. It was hot and muggy down there along the railroad service road, with the only sound, save for themselves and the sandy clopping of their horse's hooves, the occasional rattlesnake buzz of a big gray prairie grasshopper. Everything at all connected with the lynching of Dancing Dave Loman pointed to him being a not-so-innocent fellow victim of a mob that seemed to have rough justice on its side.

Unless everyone was lying, Dr. Langdon Down, Nurse Calder, and of course Rose Burnside had been wrong about at least *one* Mongoloid idiot. For a full-grown but immature-looking man who exposed any sort of erection to little colored girls seemed capable of at least a half-ass try with a pretty white lady he knew better.

On the other hand, whether the late Howard Bubblehead Burnside had deserved to be locked up in an asylum or dangled from a railroad trestle, the fact remained that a material witness to the Mongoloid's mad actions had just vanished, along with his mother, which couldn't be called rough justice or even common sense.

Nobody riding with Longarm that afternoon could come up with even a wild notion why anyone would want to kidnap little Timmy, let alone his mother. Tim Sears Senior said, "Nobody had any motive to keep you from questioning our boy, Deputy Long. His mother and me went over it all with him at breakfast, knowing you'd be asking about his encounter with the idiot in the churchyard that day. I know you may know more about asking questions. I heard you talking to those colored boys back yonder. But what's the worst thing Timmy could have told you about that crazy Bubblehead Burnside that we didn't all know already?"

Longarm said, "I keep finding out things I never knew before. By asking questions others may not have thought to ask, no offense. For example, two grown women who must have been whistled at in their time were both convinced Howard Burnside was innocent of any feelings in the dick he scared that innocent little colored gal with. Have any of you gents ever thought to delve into the secret lives of unfortunates such as Bubblehead Burnside?"

Remington Ramsay said the thought of that drooling idiot with a hard-on was sort of unsettling. Another rider opined, "It's no wonder that Sunday school teacher screamed!"

There came a general murmur of agreement. Longarm was the only one in the bunch who couldn't shake the feeling he was *missing* something. Something so simple a little boy who could barely read and write might have been able to lead the way . . . not to what, but to *who*!

Keeping his thoughts to himself, not knowing who might be listening, Longarm started cutting mental patterns in a whole new way, trying to see who'd fit them best.

Unless they'd run off together to join the circus, Timmy and his mother had been abducted, or worse, before the kid could *tell* him something. So the question before the house was not what Timmy might have known, but what he *could* have known.

Someone said the sunflower windmill out ahead was the Diamond B. Longarm wasn't sure he cared if Remington Ramsay didn't. He went on cutting patterns as they all rode on. He told himself to forget whether Bubblehead had gotten it into that poor murdered gal or not. Timmy couldn't have been an authority on such matters. He'd never said he saw his oversized playmate doing shit. It didn't matter whether that poor Mongoloid had meant to kill their Sunday school teacher or, hell, even if the dirty deed had been done by somebody else! Timmy Sears had pointed Bubblehead out. Bubblehead had been arrested for the crime and then lynched. Neither of those cowhands riding in the other way had seen anybody. But what if Bubblehead *had* been innocent and the real murderer had been afraid Timmy *might* say something to give him away?

"That would make more than one village idiot," Longarm muttered to himself. For a killer who got away clean and had them hang another in his place would have to be dumb as all get-out to risk yet another crime.

On the other hand, the prisons were filled to overflowing with old boys who just hadn't been able to resist going back for yet another raid on that same fool bank, stage line, or whatever. A man who thought your average Sunday school teacher might welcome his advances was doubtless capable of thinking a little kid was on to him.

They swung west across a cattle guard as what sounded like all those bloodhounds after Uncle Tom's daughter bayed at them for a short spell, then fell silent when somebody shrilled at them in a female voice. Longarm was still considering other patterns as he spied Fox Bancroft and some of her hands lined up on the veranda of her long sprawling sod mansion. It wasn't too clear how a murderer more cunning than most with a lot to hide fit the few solid facts they had to go on.

To begin with, abducting a small boy and a grown woman off the main shopping street in broad daylight was pushing

143

clever to impossible, and why might a killer that desperate *wait* so long?

Longarm recalled with some chagrin how he'd given any killer at the crowded coroner's inquest plenty of advance notice he was aiming to interview the kid. So the killer or killers had had all night to simply knock on the front door of the Sears house and do the whole family in, under cover of darkness, with nobody able to hazard a tight guess as to the time they did it or which way anyone might have come or gone.

He reined in, distracted, as Remington Ramsay was telling Fox Bancroft and her own riders what they were doing out her way.

Fox said, "It pains me to say it. But I can't blame it on Deacon Knox or his two sidekicks and one play-pretty. I was gracious enough to give them time to pack, and the four of them left this morning on that northbound combination. I asked."

As Longarm dismounted to tether his bay to the rail out front, he casually asked just when she and her own riders might have left town that morning.

The redhead answered just as casually, "Never left town this morning. Rode home right after you and me parted friendly after our little game of cards. It costs money to stay overnight in town, and my poor daddy never raised no fools to leave this spread to. Spent the night in my own free bed. Had Curly bed down at the livery and make sure those rascals caught that train the way I'd told 'em to. You remember Curly, don't you?"

Longarm gravely replied, "I do. You say Curly was in town this morning?"

She nodded and said, "Got home around ten. He's over to the corrals, doing Porky Shaw's old chores. Do you want to talk to him? I mean Curly, not Porky, of course."

Longarm met her mocking gaze and said, "I thought we'd agreed on Porky Shaw. I've no call to pester your new boss wrangler if he left town long before my other witness and his mother disappeared. I mean to work north of your spread and the Rocking Seven across the way to circle far and wide, scouting for sign. You know your own range, Miss Fox. I'm open to suggestions as to our best route through the trackless wilderness clear of the township.''

She said, ''You'll find such tracks as anyone left where they had to cross such sandy draws as there are in these parts. Let me rustle up fresh mounts for everybody and we just might *catch* the sons of bitches!''

But they didn't. They rode high and they rode low in a wide weary circle of close to twenty miles before they all wound up back in the Red Rooster in Pawnee Junction, convinced that nobody but a really good Pawnee war party could have carried young Timmy and his mother across all that rolling grass, dissected by ribbons of uncrossed sand. It seemed just as obvious no Indian war party had passed through Pawnee Junction in recent memory.

Once Tim Sears Senior had heard about those mysterious strangers arriving in town that morning, he demanded a house-to-house search of the whole town, insisting, ''If they never rid out with my woman and my boy, they have to be holding them somewhere here in town!''

Pronto Cross, who'd naturally joined the bunch in the Red Rooster as soon as they rode in, said soothingly, ''That ain't hardly practical, Tim. To begin with, we don't know those strangers in dark duds have done anything to anybody. I have my own boys out canvassing. They'd *been* out asking questions since early this morning. Doc Forbes says he can't issue any search warrants as the county coroner, and old Kiowa Jack says we need the circuit judge, not him or the J. P., if we want to go poking in anywhere we ain't invited.''

Fox Bancroft sipped some suds sort of daintily and suggested, ''What if we were to just spread out and ask *polite*, from door to door? Wouldn't we be able to narrow things down a heap betwixt the ones who invite us in for a look around and the ones acting as if they have something to hide?''

There came a murmur of agreement. Longarm could have pointed out that lots of folks had lots of things to hide, from dirty pictures to a just plain messy house. But he never did. For there was some merit to the redhead's casual approach to law and order. He knew half the innocent smiles around him were masking the secret thoughts of many a Minute Man. It might be interesting to let them all have some slack and see just who might find out what, doing what, and to whom. So he said he had to visit the Western Union and go home for a bite of supper, agreeing to meet up with everybody there at the Red Rooster after sundown.

He was holding out, of course. He did ride over to the Western Union, where he picked up a few answers to his earlier wires, though none told him to arrest anybody.

Then he rode back to the boardinghouse, stabled the pony he'd borrowed from the Diamond B next door, and let little Ellen Brent and the Widow MacUlric fix him up with cold meat and warmed-over soup as they asked him more questions than he had time to answer.

He told them, ''I've no idea where Mrs. Sears and her boy wound up. Whilst everyone else hunts under the rugs and compost heaps for them, I mean to search for anyone with a good reason to grab them before I could talk to the boy. Could you by any chance let me into your library after hours, Miss Ellen?''

They both knew he had a spare key on him, but the brunette smiled innocently and allowed she'd be proud to go over yonder and open up for him if he needed to read something.

He said, ''I do, ma'am. I need to look over your library copy of the county directory. You do have one, don't you?''

When she allowed they had copies of most everything ever printed in those parts he said, ''I was hoping you might. I didn't ask about the directories others might have around

Courthouse Square because I hate to have folks reading over my shoulder when I ain't sure which side they might be on.''

Ellen and Mavis MacUlric agreed they felt honored to be on his side. But Ellen was the one who wanted to screw him as soon as she had him alone over at the library after closing time.

He kissed her and fingered her some, but explained he really had wanted to study that directory before sundown. So she stamped a pretty foot and rustled it up for him, demanding, ''What do you expect to find, you brute, a signed confession from the kidnapper?''

He sat at her desk, broke his notebook out of a vest pocket, and began to write down names as he quicky moved a fingernail down the many more names of registered voters and property owners listed by the county. He was able to eliminate most right off, of course.

When he said so, Ellen wanted him to take her downstairs and show her some appreciation.

Longarm sighed and said, ''There's nothing I'd rather do tonight in the way of good clean fun, honey. But a mighty dangerous killer is loose in these parts and I have to stop him lest he kill some more. Thanks to you I've narrowed my list of possibles down a heap, but not nearly enough.''

He waved his notebook. ''When a township starts from the ground up, there's a tendency for deeply religious folks to build or rent close to the church of their persuasion, whilst folks who ain't so religious tend to send their kids to the nearest Sunday school of any church that ain't too unsettling. So I mean to start with white Anglo-Saxon surnames within a spit and a holler of First Calvinist. You can see that leaves me many a door to knock on. I might save some time in the end if I commenced with the principal of your public school. Do you know who that might be?''

She did, but said Mr. Graves was visiting kin back East while his school was closed for the summer. Longarm scowled so blackly she asked, "What did you want to ask him, Custis?"

When he told her, she laughed and said, "Oh, that's easy. I told you the school and this library were under the same school board here in Pawnee Junction. We naturally keep their old records down in our cellar, having ever so much more room. What did you want to look up? I don't think that Mongoloid idiot ever attended our public school here in town."

Longarm was already on his way with her desk lamp, saying, "I know for a fact poor Howard Burnside was never allowed anywhere but that nice gal's Sunday school. This awkwardly long list includes all the gents with the first name Howard who live an easy walk from First Calvinist. Gents tend to name their oldest boy after themselves. I might narrow things down more if I listed just the possible Howards with poor school records or, better yet, expulsion records. A big dumb white boy looks like a big dumb white boy to colored kids who might be afraid of him."

She followed him down the stairs, saying, "But I thought that little Timmy said he saw a bigger boy named Howard that awful day at the church and . . . Oh, good heavens, you're so clever I could just eat you all up!"

He felt sort of clever himself by the time he'd pawed through a lot of old report cards to narrow his list down to a dozen. So he showed his appreciation for the helpful little gal dog-style on that nearby army cot before he left just at sundown.

There just wasn't time to let her eat him all up, dad blast it.

Chapter 19

Longarm found young Howard Simmons sitting out front on the porch with his parents in the gloaming as things cooled off and the first wishing star winked on above.

He introduced himself to Howard Simmons Senior, and said he'd like a word alone with the big fourteen-year-old about some other kids who might have been up to some mischief.

The Simmons boy went willingly with Longarm out to the front gate. Longarm smiled down in the gathering dusk and said, "I reckon you know why I've come for you, Howard. I'd talked to Nero, Calvin, and that little colored gal you scared that time, just funning with her."

The kid was either a mighty fine actor who'd flunked the fifth grade, or he meant it when he said, "I don't know no Nero Calhoun and my folks don't allow me to play with colored kids."

Longarm said, "Timmy Sears says he saw you coming out of First Calvinist the day Miss Mildred got hurt. You want to tell me about that?"

The normal-looking but likely slow-witted youth brightened and replied, "Oh, you're talking about that Sunday school teacher who got stabbed by the Chinee! I heard my elders talking about that. I don't know why anybody says he saw *me* at her church. I go to Saint Paul's Lutheran.''

Longarm led him back to the porch and told his parents the boy had been a great help to him. Then he got out of there before they could ask him how. He checked his list under a street lamp to forge on. But he had much the same luck three more times with other Howards, then at the home of a Howard Masterson who'd named his only son after old John Brown of Kansas.

Then he came to where the widowed Mrs. Howard Tendring lived all alone with her only child, Howard Tendring III. When the poor old widow woman came to her front door by candlelight, she turned out to be a right handsome brunette in her late thirties, with one hell of a set of legs under her, judging by the soft light shining through her thin pongee robe. She looked flustered and said that she hadn't been expecting gentlemen callers. Longarm ticked the brim of his hat to her and said he was sorry to drop by on a lady after she'd let her hair down for the night, but that he was the law and that he had to talk to her boy, Howard.

She called back over her shoulder to the lad who'd been expelled from school for bullying the smaller kids and threatening his teacher. As they waited she said, ''I hope he hasn't done anything wrong again. I spoke to him sharply about teasing that little colored girl, and he promised me he'd never do it again.''

Longarm never let on her words were news to him. He calmly asked who'd come to her about that accusation. He wasn't at all surprised when she told him Pronto Cross himself had warned her he'd have to run the boy in if he ever did anything like that again.

When Howard Tendring III loomed in the candlelight behind his far prettier mother, Longarm could see why smaller kids were tense around him. The weak-chinned lout with eyebrows that met in the middle stood over six feet tall on

150

his bare feet and had fists as big as your average blacksmith. He was dressed in jeans and gray undershirt. So Longarm allowed a private chat on the front steps would do.

The sullen-looking kid stepped out, and his mother left their front door open but stepped away from it inside. So Longarm was free to ask the same trick questions. But when he started by saying he'd just come from seeing little Timmy Sears, the sudden flash of candle glow on steel was all that saved him!

Longarm sucked in his gut as he crawfished from a sweeping stab that would have done old Jim Bowie proud. As he felt the end rail of the porch with the cheeks of his ass, he saw the concealed weapon was almost as long and surely as sharp as your average Bowie knife. So he grabbed the big kid's wrist at the end of the second swing and slapped open-handed, hard, with his free palm.

Howard Tendring III let go of the knife and started running, barefoot, into the night. He crashed through his mother's picket fence and just kept running, with Longarm close behind.

Longarm had long legs and less worry about where he planted his pounding heels in the dark. But the barefoot boy out ahead was wild with sheer terror and as anxious to get away as Longarm was to catch him. So damned if the distance between them didn't seem to grow wider as Longarm struggled to get the cuffs off the back of his gun rig on the fly and willed his fool legs to run faster.

Then a female voice cried out through the night, "I'll hold him and you brand him, Custis!"

So that was about what they did. Fox Bancroft roped damned fine for a woman throwing sideways at a lope in such tricky light. Her loop snapped tight as she slid her pony to a calf-busting squat on its haunches, and Howard Tendring III was flat on his ass in the roadside weeds before he could free himself from her oiled and braided hemp.

Then Longarm was on top of the writhing and cussing

young monster, and it was still a near thing, taking such a spiteful kicking spitter without busting his damned skull.

Fox Bancroft helped by keeping her line tight as the throw-rope pinned the youth's powerful arms to his sides. Longarm came close to singing soprano for a spell when the unruly schoolboy kicked hard, with skill, but only bruised a thigh.

Then Longarm had the mean young shit face-down with his hands cuffed behind him. He grabbed a fistful of dark hair and banged the kid's face against the ground a couple of times as he told him firmly but not unkindly to cut it out before somebody got hurt.

The nearby mounted redhead asked for her rope back. So Longarm loosened the noose and slipped it off over the kid's head as he knelt on sweet Howard's spine. Fox Bancroft was whipping in and recoiling when Mrs. Tendring came shrilling down the path, weeping and wailing about her precious child.

She was still in her thin robe, and she sure smelled nice as she hugged Longarm from behind, her tits rubbing all over the back of his vest while she said there was some mistake and that she'd do anything, anything, if only he'd let her darling boy go.

Then Fox Bancroft had dismounted to join them, saying, "Go home and put some clothes on, Felicia Tendring. This federal lawman never would have come for your foul-mouthed brat if he hadn't *done* something. What did her foul-mouthed brat do, Custis? We've been looking all over for you since you never came back to tell us what happened to that other kid and his own mother."

Longarm rose to his feet with Howard Tendring III, despite the combined efforts of mother and son, as he soberly said, "You have to eat the apple a bite at a time. I don't reckon this boy knows what happened to that other boy. You don't know where we might find your young friend Timmy, do you, Howard?"

To which his young prisoner replied with a sob, "Screw

152

Timmy Sears. Screw all of you! You're all against me! All of you! Everybody hates me and I hate everybody, so there!''

Felicia Tendring gasped, let go of Longarm from behind, and came around his front to slap the kid's face.

Her son spat, ''Don't you go hitting on me, Mom! I'll *cut* you if you hit me like that again!''

His mother covered her face with her hands and began to bawl like a frightened baby. Fox Bancroft softly said, ''Go home and put those clothes on. You can talk to your boy later, after things have calmed down. You're taking him to the town marshal's now, aren't you, Deputy Long?''

Longarm had been thinking about that. He said, ''The sheriff's county jail is built more solid and fireproof. I reckon I'll turn him in to the county and see where they want to go from there. There don't seem any just cause to charge him with anything federal. We'd have a time proving he had anything to do with the death of Dancing Dave Loman, and the murder of Mildred Powell is a matter for your own grand jury to decide.''

Fox Bancroft gasped, ''You're charging *this* kid with that crime? I thought Mildred Powell was attacked by Bubblehead Burnside! Didn't little Timmy Sears say he *saw* that feeble-minded cuss coming out of the cellar door whilst the dying gal was still screaming inside?''

Longarm said, ''No. Not if you read over the transcript of his kid talk carefully. Timmy said he saw *Howard* at the scene of the crime. So they added two and two to get seven when they asked if he didn't mean Bubblehead. Timmy was likely telling the simple truth, as he saw it, when he simply told them a generous-hearted young lady had told them never to use the cruel nickname Bubblehead for *another Howard entirely*!''

Felicia Tendring told her baby she'd get dressed and go see a friend or lawyer called George about his plight. As she turned away she sweetly added, ''Don't sign anything. Don't

153

tell them anything, honey. Uncle George and I will have you out in no time!"

As she scurried away in her slippers, Longarm turned to Fox and quietly asked, "Uncle George?"

The redhead shrugged and said, "Ask *this* one. George is a more common name than Howard. How did you figure out that this was the Howard little Timmy really meant, by the way?"

Longarm said, "It's a long story. I'll tell you along the way as we march this one over to the county jail."

So she led her paint pony afoot as the two of them escorted the handcuffed Howard Tendring III the quarter mile or less to the jail. When Longarm got to how he'd had trouble buying a sweet-natured and baby-sexed Mongoloid as a slashing sex maniac who'd exposed himself to a younger gal earlier, Howard Tendring III complained, "I never just *supposed* nothing. I meant to *give* 'em what I knew they both wanted. But they were teasing me, like alley cats in heat, smiling dirty and then trying to twist away at the last minute!"

Fox Bancroft softly gasped, "Oh, my God!"

Longarm told the monster, "Your mother told you to save your tales of woe for your family lawyer, Howard. Old Kiowa Jack or somebody from his office will take down all you have to say for yourself while your mother and your lawyer listen in, see?"

Other folks were coming out to their front gates as Longarm and the well-known local stockwoman passed on foot with the neighborhood bully. Fox Bancroft asked why the little shit couldn't spill his guts along the way if he was of a mind to.

Longarm said, "Confession is good for the soul, but it can play hob with the prosecution in a delicate case. I don't mean this here slashing Romeo is delicate. I means he's underage and they're going to try to sell the jury on his being *loco en la cabeza*. I never might have come anywhere close

154

to him if he and some other Howards hadn't been mighty slow and bothersome in your public school.''

She made a wry face and said, ''I sure feel sorry for poor Rose Burnside. We thought her kid brother, Bubblehead, was the only village idiot we had to worry about. Can you imagine how she must have felt when they came for him, refusing to believe her when she swore he couldn't be the one they were after?''

Longarm said, ''Nope. Neither can you. Nobody but Miss Rose will ever know what it felt like to have that particular sweet and harmless problem child of voting age on her hands.''

Closer to the center of town, they were joined by Tim Sears Senior and Remington Ramsay. The hardware man said, ''We heard you caught up with somebody down this way and, good grief, is that the Tendring boy you seem to have arrested there?''

Longarm replied, ''Yep. I had to. The charge is murder most foul and attempted rape. This is the Howard little Timmy meant.''

The missing child's father shook a fist in the young prisoner's face and demanded, ''What have you done with my wife and child, you murderous simp?''

Howard Tendring III told him to go screw himself. Longarm blocked the outraged father's backhand swing, and the big strong hardware man pulled Sears away, soothing him the way you calmed a spooked critter.

Longarm said, ''I doubt he knows, Tim. Help us get him over to the county jail and we'll study on who's holding your wife and your boy.''

As the growing procession moved on, it was Remington Ramsay who asked what Longarm had in mind about the missing mother and son.

Longarm sighed and said, ''If I knew anything for certain, I'd be proud to share it with you. By the way, did you know what all that railroad paper on Mavis MacUlric's walls is

155

worth? *I* do because I wired a railroad stock slicker about Credit Mobilier earlier.''

The hardware mogul said, ''It's not really that good for papering walls. I offered her par value on the matured bonds. She's too smart to think a construction company pays dividends to shareholders after it's been out of business for years.''

Before Longarm could ask why anyone would want to pay anything for any worthless railroad paper, they were joined by Pronto Cross who demanded, ''What on earth are you doing with this lad in handcuffs? I know young Howard and his family, Longarm! He may be a tad unruly, but you can't be serious about him kidnapping Timmy Sears!''

The big kid lowered his face, as if ashamed to be seen by anyone he knew, as Longarm said, ''Ain't holding him on kidnapping. It will be up to your local courts to decide, after I turn him in to them, but I'd say he's an easy win for murder in the first, whether little Timmy can testify against him or not. If push comes to shove, I can come up with three other kids who stand ready to identify him as the one Timmy meant when he mentioned his overgrown playmate Howard.''

Pronto Cross said, ''Oh, Lord, I'd best rustle up more help whilst you get him over to the jail, and bar all the outside doors and windows. For whether you are right or wrong, there's liable to be hell to pay as soon as the Minute Men learn they might have hung the wrong half-wit the other night!''

Chapter 20

Sheriff Wigan's two deputies were surprised, but willing to hold young Howard Tendring till their boss got back to town to tell them differently. The kid still refused to talk politely to anybody but his momma or his Uncle George. When one of the deputies backhanded him, Longarm said, "Leave him be. His mother and her lawyer, lover, or whatever ought to be along any time now."

So they locked him up in one of the patent cells and commenced to douse the inside lamps and get set for anyone else who might come to call that evening.

Fox Bancroft asked Longarm which window he wanted her to man. He said, "No offense, but you ain't a man, and seeing you have that pony out front, I've got a better chore for you."

He ripped two pages out of his notebook and spread them on a windowsill to jot hasty messages by the light of the street lamp outside.

Handing them to the redhead, he explained, "I'd be obliged if you could send these wires for me at the Western Union and not show 'em to anyone else you meet along the way."

She started to argue, nodded soberly, and left Longarm, the two sheriff's deputies, and Remington Ramsay feeling sort of lonesome in the county jail.

Ramsay joined Longarm at the open window near the bolted front door to muse, "Pronto could be wrong. It's not as if they had anyone all that ambitious egging them on. I'm pretty sure Porky Shaw was the main ringleader last time, and everyone on both sides knows what you did to Porky Shaw."

Longarm said, "Porky had a pal with a ten-gauge Greener who shot up my room. Nobody on the side of the law has seen fit to tell me who he is. Let's talk about *him*, Ramsay."

The big hardware man said, "The reason I told Mavis MacUlric I'd buy her worthless railroad bonds at par is that I *tried* to help her when I first heard she was having financial trouble. She acted like I was trying to buy her fair white body, for Chrissake!"

"Weren't you?" asked Longarm dryly.

Ramsay snapped, "Damn it, my intentions are pure toward Mavis MacUlric. I've never had the time or inclination to chase skirts for the hell of it. I was true to my late wife while she lasted, and I was there when Martin MacUlric died of that heart stroke after his own long and happy marriage."

"That made you hot for his widow?" demanded Longarm, who'd noticed on his own that Mavis MacUlric wasn't suffering from warts on her nose or a flat chest.

Ramsay said, "Call me hardheaded when it comes to romance. But a man with horse sense can fall for a handsome woman who's been proven a good wife as easy as he can fall for a spinster schoolmarm or some divorced gal who might well have been the one in the wrong!"

"I'm sure you and Miss Mavis will be very happy," Longarm replied in a dismissive tone. "I never asked about your love life. I asked for some straight talk about those Minute Men. Before you say you don't know shit, I read that book you had printed up about the carving of this whole county from a howling wilderness. Are you now trying to say you were never invited to join?"

The still-young old-timer of the Sand Hill Country smiled thinly and confessed, "I might have been doing some of the inviting, if you want to hear about the Cheyenne Scare of '78."

He stared out at the ominously empty and dimly lit courthouse square as he added in a softer tone, "My God, it seems like yesterday. But the county was half as settled and barely incorporated. The state capital at Lincoln seemed so far away and those renegade Cheyenne were said to be so close!"

Longarm firmly stated, "Dull Knife and his breakaway band would have headed for a leper colony before they'd get within a day's ride of that nearby Pawnee Agency. Aside from that, they weren't wearing paint and the last thing they were looking for was another fight with *our* kind."

He got out two cheroots and handed one to the hardware man as he added morosely, "They got one just the same, when the army caught up with 'em over to the west. You hardy pioneers organized your own half-ass militia to fight *Indians*?"

Ramsay waited until Longarm had lit his cheroot for him before he explained, "Just for that one emergency. I'm afraid it was my own idea to call us Minute Men. As a history buff I was thinking of how the real Minute Men had been organized back in the 1700s to deal with an earlier red menace. We disbanded the next spring, of course."

Longarm blew smoke out his nostrils and demanded, "What was Porky Shaw, a slow reader?"

Ramsay sighed and said, "That's exactly how you could describe him and some few of the others in these parts. Militia meetings are *fun* when there's no war on. I had a serious business to run. Most of the others who'd started the Minute Men with me dropped out for much the same reasons. Sitting around a campfire with jugs seems less attractive to men with serious chores to occupy their hands and minds."

"Then how come you respectable folk here in Pawnee Junction refuse to tell the law who's left in the ragged-ass bunch that's left?"

Ramsay shrugged and replied, "It's more that you're an outsider than the fact that you're a lawman. Everyone in town likely suspects a few friends and neighbors still meet in secret to ride at night. Nobody who's no longer an active member could say for *sure* who might be doing what, and to be fair, most of the times the Minute Men have taken the law in their own hands, they've gone after someone who had it coming."

"You don't have a town marshal or a county sheriff, huh?" Longarm demanded dryly.

The local man said, "You can see what sort of sheriff we have. Old Wigan is a political hack who spends more time down at his local party headquarters in Ogallala than here, when he's not goldbricking with his in-laws out to the Rocking Seven."

"What about Pronto Cross?" asked Longarm, adding, "I understand your board of aldermen paid good money to import a town-tamer with a rep."

Ramsay said, "We did. I was there and I voted for the motion. Pronto Cross has calmed our Saturday nights in town considerable and nobody has insulted a woman in public for quite a spell. But I hardly have to tell a lawman how many times the statute laws just don't seem to apply to a total son of a bitch."

Longarm nodded soberly and said, "You're talking about habitual mean drunks, wife beaters, untidy neighbors in general. This may come as a shock, but neighborhood vigilante gangs always seem to start out as a means of dealing with pests the regular law can't seem to cope with."

He blew more smoke out his nostrils and snorted, "They go from whupping wife beaters to burning out suspected stock thieves or lynching unpopular suspects. You ain't ready to tell me who's in charge now, right?"

Ramsay said, "Wrong. I just don't *know*. I'm only half sure about a few of the lesser lights. I think one of my yard hands is still a member. He said he wasn't there when they lynched Bubblehead Burnside. I asked. That's not saying anyone told me the truth."

Longarm spotted the willowy form of Fox Bancroft striding afoot across the square with two taller figures, both male, one town and one country.

All three were packing repeating carbines at port arms. Longarm unbolted the front door to let them in anyway.

The cowhand backing his redheaded boss was the kid they called Curly. Longarm was just as glad Curly hadn't chosen the other side. His saddle gun was a seven-shot Spencer .52, and he wore a six-gun on his right hip.

The other man who'd crossed the square with the gal was the skinny printer Preston of the *Pawnee Junction Advertiser*. He said he'd always wanted to be a newspaper reporter instead of a type sticker, and added that the mob had been gathering in the Red Rooster when Pronto Cross had come in and read them the riot act. Preston couldn't say where they'd gone after the town marshal dispersed them from the saloon. The newspaperman was packing a Winchester '73. The gal had a somewhat older but just as deadly Winchester Yellowboy with brass receiver.

She said she'd sent his wires and ordered yet another loyal hand to ride out to the Diamond B for additional help.

Preston said, "Oh, please, Lord, let me live through this first big scoop as the snowballs start flying. Where do you want me posted, Uncle Sam?"

Longarm told the well-armed newspaperman to watch the next window over, and moved back through the darkness to reorganize their defenses now that he had seven gun muzzles to position. He figured Curly, Sears, and the two sheriff's deputies could hold the more solid back. Anyone rushing the rear door would have one avenue of approach across the stable yard, thanks to brick walls running back to the stable and carriage house. But it was black as a bitch out yonder until one of the deputies suggested, and Longarm approved, lighting an outside lamp that hung facing them from the stable wall. Nobody on either side would be able to put it out without exposing himself in the open. A marksman could doubtless shoot it out from inside the jail, but it seemed safe from anyone hitting it with a bullet around a corner.

Longarm rejoined the three others up front. There were no side windows through the thick brick walls for anyone to shoot in or out through. Longarm posted Ramsay and the newspaperman on the far side of the front door. He told Fox Bancroft to stay closer to him, and chided her gently for ever coming back.

She said, "I told you I sent for my riders out to the Diamond B, and I have to be with my men when they get here, don't I?"

Longarm sighed and said, "Those riders who ain't riding with your local Minute Men, you mean. Ramsay just owned up that he suspects one of *his* hired hands. The trouble with these secret societies is that they're so blamed *secret*. You say you got them wires off for me?"

She said she had, adding, "My boys will be here long before those state troopers or the federal deputies from Ogallala could hope to make it!"

The newspaperman on the far side of the front door, who seemed to be taking notes, opined, "They'd better get here even sooner, for yonder comes our sort of determined-looking neighborhood uplifting society and . . . Sweet Jesus, I didn't know we had that many interested in one rotten kid!"

Longarm snubbed out his smoke on the sill as he counted roughly two platoons coming across the square in a line of skirmish, with waving torches as well as hooded masks. Remington Ramsay softly called out, "I knew it. Feed sack or no feed sack, I recognize the patched overalls of that rascal who works for me. I mean, that rascal who *used* to work for me.''

Longarm called back, ''Douse that smoke and let them guess where to aim. Don't challenge the one you recognize by name unless I ask you to. Mobs are like bananas. They're yellow and like to hang in a bunch. Once you single a cuss out, he's inclined to back down or come at you sudden. I want you all to let me do the talking, hear?''

Nobody argued. Longarm's mouth felt a mite dry too as he watched the ragged line of fifty-odd masked men advancing at a slow but steady pace.

He growled, ''Ain't near a tenth of the grown men in and about your dinky town, Ramsay. Where's all the *rest* of 'em? You reckon they're *scared* of our brave little band of big bad bully boys?''

Ramsay answered simply, ''Yes. As a history buff I can tell you a heap of history would read different if all the little kids stood up to the bully boys who smoke corn silk and bust windows. The bully breed gets the hex on the rest of us early, because *our* mommas teach us to be nice before they ever send us to school to meet up with meaner brats.''

''Reminds me of the one we got locked up in the back,'' said Longarm. ''It's sort of odd how gents with no respect for law and order seem so anxious to string up outlaws.''

He told everyone to get ready to move out of line with his or her dark window before he cocked his .44-40 and called out, ''That's about close enough, boys. Who's in charge and what's this all about?''

A Minute Man standing close to another with a sawed-off, double-barrel ten-gauge aimed politely, called out, ''You know what we're here for, Longarm. We want the murderous half-wit who murdered Mildred Powell. We don't want no judge saying you can't hang mean kids!''

To which Longarm replied in a disgusted tone, ''Do tell? I thought you boys had already done that. How many times were you planning on hanging a prisoner on the same charge, with no warrant and no trial?''

His words seemed to fall on ears made deaf by hard liquor as well as earlier orations, judging from the angry rumbles up and down the line.

Another voice called, ''Hand him over. Now. Unless you was planning on doing the rope dance beside him!''

Longarm called back, ''I've sent for both state and federal lawmen, speaking of rope dances. If I were you boys I'd quit whilst I was ahead. You've already got the blood of a harmless half-wit on your hands. If you can't see Bubblehead Burnside was innocent, what in blue blazes do you want with young Howard Tendring?''

He could tell from some puzzled murmurs that he'd scored a point. So he drew a bead on that one with the Greener shotgun as he called out cheerfully, ''Go home and let the judge and jury decide which one of them it was.''

Then he took a deep breath and called, ''All but you, Pronto Cross. I want you to drop that gun and step this way with your hands filled with sky!''

It was just as well he'd yelled that well back and to one side. For the one holding the ten-gauge wasn't the one who swung a Winchester muzzle up to bore a whole lot of holes through the blackness Longarm was just to one side of. Then Longarm fired back at a clear target illuminated by street lamp and torchlight before the one with the ten-gauge could come unstuck and blast away with both barrels.

By then, of course, Longarm had moved down to the next window to shove Fox Bancroft to the safety of the floor as both Remington Ramsay and Preston fired at the shotgun man, to flop him screaming and kicking across the face-down form of the treacherous bastard Longarm had just killed.

Then things got noisy as all get-out for a spell.

Chapter 21

It got tougher to hit targets that were crawfishing away from you and filling the air between with the gunsmoke of their return fire. So as the redcoats had noticed at Lexington Green (according to old Remington Ramsay later) you could fire right into a raggedy mob and only lay a handful on the ground before they'd retreated clean out of sight.

As the smoke cleared, nine figures and a whole lot of smoldering torches lay strewn across the otherwise empty square. From the way at least four of them were flopping and moaning, they'd likely live.

Longarm was glad. Dead men tell no tales, and he still had a lot of loose ends to wrap up around these parts.

The same natural feelings that kept most from standing up to the scowling and swaggering seemed to encourage the sweeter-natured pups to snap at the heels of a big bad wolf in retreat with its old tail between its legs. So in no time at all the square began to fill up some more with a more jovial crowd.

Longarm said, "Cover me," and stepped out, .44-40 in hand, to move out as far as the ones they'd dropped closer to the front door. Fox Bancroft tagged along uninvited. He hadn't ordered her to cover him from the jail, she explained demurely.

He smiled thinly and rolled the one who'd had the ten-gauge off the face-down leader of the mob. He hunkered to remove the mask and expose the face of a total stranger—to him, at least.

Then the redhead who hailed from those parts gasped and said she knew him. He was Swen Bergen, who ran the municipal corral across from Longarm's boardinghouse.

Longarm allowed that answered more than one question, and reached out to yank the pillowcase off the head and shoulders of the late Pronto Cross. The erstwhile town marshal and mob leader was staring up surprised as hell about being dead.

Longarm wasn't nearly as surprised as Fox Bancroft. She gasped, "Oh, what a two-faced liar! He only dispersed that crowd from the Red Rooster so he could take command and lead them against us on the sly! He reminds me of a boy I went to school with, only worse! But how did you know, Custis? I heard you call his very name, just as he opened up on you, the dumb thing!"

Longarm said, "When a man keeps telling you things that just don't seem to make sense, you commence to suspect he must be lying to you. When a man *keeps* lying to you, you begin to suspect he must be hiding something from you. He didn't want me paying enough mind to *him* to get suspicious, so he told me mysterious strangers had got off the train from Ogallala. Had he thought tighter about his made-up menace, he'd have had this other rogue say they'd hired some livery stock. But he must have taken me for simple. He never accounted for them riding off or having any place to stay in such a small town."

As they strode over toward another downed Minute Man, Longarm added, "Pronto said he'd seen his mysterious strangers getting off the morning train. But *you* told me you posted your own rider, Curly, to make sure those crooked gamblers got aboard that same northbound train to *leave* town. So that left me with conflicting stories, unless poor Pronto here or Curly inside needed eyeglasses.''

As he hunkered down to unmask the swamper from the Red Rooster, the redheaded gal gasped, ''Remind me never to fib to you! For you surely do pay attention, and as soon as one does, it doesn't make sense that the town law would notice possible outlaws getting off a train whilst my poor country boy Curly would pay no mind to a couple of sinister total strangers after I'd told him to keep his eyes peeled!''

The swamper was dead too. As Longarm straightened up, he spied Doc Forbes kneeling by a moaning cowhand his redheaded local guide knew as a rider off the Lazy Four to the southeast.

Longarm called out, ''I need at least one in shape to talk when my fellow lawmen get off the train, Doc.''

Doc Forbes called back, ''I can promise you three. Too early to say about Ned Danfield. One of you spine-shot him serious! Lord knows what an accountant was doing over this way with a fool sack over his head!''

Felicia Tendring, young Howard's weeping mother, was coming their way, fully dressed, with a pasty-faced cuss in an undertaker's suit who allowed he was the family lawyer.

The nice-looking mother of the really ugly-natured Howard Tendring III stared wildly about at the results of the short savage gunfight and blazed, ''What have you done to my baby, you monster?''

Longarm ticked the brim of his hat to her and said, ''Just saved his neck for the time being, ma'am.''

He turned to call out to his pals inside the jail, ''Let the monster's mother and Uncle George talk to him through the bars. I'll be joining you directly, lest these other monsters demand a rematch!''

As he hunkered to identify another downed Minute Man, this one still breathing but unconscious, Fox Bancroft said,

"You told me you'd caught Pronto in more than one big fib, Custis."

Longarm called out, "Hey, Doc? When you got time I got another live one for you here."

Then he straightened up and waved his gun muzzle toward the front door of the jail to herd the redhead that way as he explained, "His second unlikely tale was the one he told about little Timmy Sears and his mother. He told me the night of the coroner's inquest that he'd have the boy over to his office the following morning for me to talk to. He did go to the boy's house, and like Tim Senior inside says, they did agree to have little Timmy meet up with me at the town marshal's office."

As they strode together toward the county jail, Longarm swore under his breath and said, "I had no reason to suspect a known town-tamer with a good rep at the time. But I still wish I'd gone direct to the poor little kid's home and to blazes with his bedtime. But I had no call to suspect skull-duggery before Pronto told me, barefaced, how they'd been waiting for me at his office but stepped out to run some other errands in the middle of town."

Fox Bancroft nodded soberly and said, "I was there when you all rode out to my spread, searching for the boy and his mother. But try as we might, we never cut sign as we searched for the missing pair and those strangers who'd likely . . . But Custis, if Curly never saw any sinister strangers getting off any train . . ."

"That's about the size of it," Longarm said grimly. The heavy door ahead gaped open for them as he added, "Unless Pronto's local and likely innocent deputies were lying about a whole mess of local merchants and shopping folks, who'd have had to be lying instead? Not a living soul but Pronto Cross himself said they'd seen little Timmy and his poor mother leave the town lockup to do spit. Women and children don't vanish into thin air on the streets of their own hometown in the middle of a workday. So like I said, as I tried in vain to find anyone else who'd back old Pronto's unlikely stories, I commenced to get suspicious. He cinched it for me earlier this evening when he gave us some feeble excuse to run off some more as I was arresting yet another murderer of a town gal who'd been murdered *within his jurisdiction!* He didn't seem to be around here the night the Minute Men came for that poor Burnside boy and, well, I may be slow but I do plod on till I plow up *something.*"

They stepped inside. Remington Ramsay asked if he thought it was over. Longarm said he thought it might be. But he wanted to hold the place tight until those state and federal lawmen arrived.

He said, "They'll likely ask the railroad to run them up here from the main line aboard a special. It ain't as if they have to worry about the tracks ahead, once that southbound I just missed gets down yonder in an hour or so."

Tim Sears Senior came out from the back, almost sobbing, "That mean Tendring kid just told his mother and her lawyer that my boy had nothing to do with the murder of Mildred Powell. But why was our Timmy hanging about with that full-grown half-wit to begin with?"

Longarm told him gently, "Howard Tendring couldn't get boys his own age to hang about with him. He and Timmy weren't as far apart in mental prowess as they might have looked, walking railroad tracks and such. Your boy was naturally more innocent and less interested in why little boys and little gals were built different. I doubt anything you'd have to feel ashamed of took place. The big girl-crazy lout was paying less attention to a tag-along kid than the tag-along kid was paying to him."

The worried father said, "We should have kept a tighter eye on our Timmy. Have you any idea where that two-faced Pronto Cross had been holding my wife and child, Deputy Long?"

Longarm nodded soberly and softly replied, "I wish there was some nicer way to say it, Tim. But Pronto Cross didn't want your son to talk to me. So I fear we're never going to find either your boy or his mother alive.''

Tim Sears Senior staggered as if he'd been punched in the head, and Fox Bancroft grabbed hold of him in a motherly way while she called Longarm an unfeeling brute.

Longarm nodded soberly and replied, ''None of us here can feel Tim's pain. Pronto Cross got off way too easy. But saying it never happened ain't going to unhappen it, and we still have to find their remains.''

Tim Sears Senior sobbed, ''My God, that son of a bitch could have buried them easy anywhere for miles around in those infernal sand hills!''

Longarm shook his head and pointed out, ''No, he couldn't. He'd have had to sneak them out of a busy town in broad day, and I for one would have noticed any buckboard he was driving.''

Turning to Remington Ramsay, he asked, ''Is it possible you were the contractor who threw up the marshal's office along with all the other public buildings, Oh, Pioneer?''

Ramsay nodded easily and said, ''Sure, at cost. But before you ask, there are no secret rooms, nor space to sneak in one's own, over at our modest town lockup.''

Longarm quietly asked, ''Might it have a cellar, like your library?''

Ramsay said it did. Tim Sears Senior gasped, ''Oh, Dear Lord!'' and broke free of Fox Bancroft to dash out the front door. The redhead cried, ''Now see what you've done, you unfeeling beast!'' and tore out across the square after him.

The newspaperman, Preston, dithered, ''I don't know whether to run after them or stay here! I'm afraid I'll miss out on the big story no matter what I do!''

Longarm smiled wearily and said, ''Chase after them, but do me a favor and gather up Doc Forbes along the way. I hope I'm wrong. But if I'm right, an official coroner's report will sure come in handy.''

As the newspaperman left, Longarm turned to Ramsay and

said, "My boss calls that delegating authority. He likes it when I get other lawmen to co-sign my notes. Sometimes they read sort of complicated."

Then he fished out two more cheroots as he added, "This one ain't as complicated as some cases I've been sent out on. But old Billy Vail will be pleased to have my uncertain spelling backed up by Doc Forbes and less sneaky local lawmen."

Curly came out from the back to say that the lawyer wanted to talk to him. Longarm said, "Tell him he can talk to me out here. I ain't trying to be rude. I hope it's over. But if it ain't, I've already saved young Howard's guilty neck for him this evening!"

When the cowhand left, Ramsay took a drag on his second free smoke and said, "You were saying you didn't find all this confusing. I'll be buttered with axle grease and dipped in shit if I can see what in the devil Pronto Cross was up to! Nobody ever gave him permit to set up and lead any second county militia, and even if he wanted to, why would he have wanted to? He was already the town law, for Chrissake!"

Longarm took a drag on his own cheroot as he morosely stared out at the townsfolk gathering up dead and wounded they knew better than he could hope to. He said, "Pronto Cross was an old hand at taming cow towns and keeping them sedate. Like Sheriff Wigan, he knew that even though they send lawmen like me after the really wild and woolly riders of the Owlhoot Trail, policing a mixed bag of town and country drunks can be dangerous as hell whether you do it too firm or too gentle. If you rule the roost with a firmer hand than called for, you make heaps of enemies and get fired a lot, like poor old proddy James Butler Hickok did before he got backshot by Cockeyed Jack McCall."

He blew a smoke ring and continued. "Tame a town just a tad too gentle, the way Marshal Tom Smith tamed Abilene a few years ago, and you can wind up shot by a trash-white like Andy McConnell and killed with an axe by the shiftless

171

Moses Miles. So your Sheriff Wigan and Pronto worked out a gentleman's agreement. The sheriff would leave the township drunks to Pronto, Pronto would leave the country drunks to the sheriff's tender mercies, and the Minute Men would deal with anyone really dangerous. No kith or kin was likely to come after a lawman if that particular lawman hadn't done anything to him. Meanwhile, the taxpayers couldn't fault a lawman for tolerating a wild man who'd finally been run out of town or worse by unknown vigilantes, see?''

Ramsay sighed and said, ''I do now. Are you saying even our lazy old sheriff was party to this devil's bargain?''

Longarm shrugged and replied, ''Well, it's agreed he seemed sort of lazy when he should have been upholding the law. We'll find out how deep a part he played in any lynching as soon as we've had time to question the surviving Minute Men. I expect they'll be easier to question, now that they've lost their leaders and their masks.''

He blew another smoke ring and added tolerantly, considering what they'd just gone through with the sons of bitches, ''I expect we'll find old Pronto Cross had the final say, before and after I shot it out with that loudmouthed Porky Shaw. Pronto had the best motive for running a tame mob, so he could avoid having to stand up alone to real wild men. But you were right about it being a bargain with the devil. Any lawman who thinks it's practical to break the law to uphold it is just about as practical as a fool who sets his house on fire to keep warm. But I reckon few such gents have ever read that tale about Dr. Faust and Mr. Mephistopheles. For every time we make a bargain with the devil, it turns out to be a dumb one.''

Chapter 22

That expected special combination rolled in just after midnight with four federal deputies, a detachment of state troopers, and a declaration of martial law.

By that time the pathetic remains of little Timmy Sears and his murdered mother had been recovered from their shallow grave in the clay floor of the cellar of the town marshal's office. Doc Forbes said they'd both been killed with a small hammer they found in the marshal's desk upstairs.

So the surviving members of the Pawnee Junction Minute Men were falling over one another to make sworn depositions about all their recent night riding. A lot of what they had to say for themselves was self-serving guff, but some of it was sincere, and all of it was easy enough to check because nobody now had any use for a two-face who'd murder a mother and child to cover his mistake about Bubblehead.

As others came forward to tell tales about the now-discredited and no-longer-feared Minute Men, it developed that Pronto Cross and a handful of close pals had been using and abusing both the Minute Men themselves and a lot of local merchants. It was Longarm who was able to detail the way their protection flimflam worked, because he'd run across it before in New Orleans, where those immigrant gangs they called Black Handers sold the same bill of goods to worried minds.

Some of the recent Minute Men seemed vexed as all get-out to learn they hadn't been let in on the extorted cash, goods, and services in spite of their being used to scare folks.

Longarm pointed out that the common soldiers who'd won the southwest third of the country from Mexico hadn't been paid the current going rate of thirteen and beans a month. He was used to getting the short end of the stick.

That was why he never complained as the pushy deputies out of the nearby Ogallala District Court took over the investigation as if they'd been there all the time. Longarm hadn't planned on growing old and gray in the sand hills of Nebraska, and there was a lot to be said for letting others do the leg-and paperwork as long as you were content to let them hog the glory.

Longarm knew his own home office would have to allow he'd done as much as he'd been sent to do, even more, once his federal prisoner had been left in no shape to stand trial in Denver. And he hadn't been shoved aside nearly as rudely as the local township and county powers.

Longarm hadn't had to point out that Pronto Cross couldn't have been the only local official in cahoots with the highly irregular vigilante riders. The major in charge of the state troopers had only had to hear the Minute Men had been secretly led by the town marshal before he stripped every official in the county of all powers, pro tem, and said everyone could consider their fool selves occupied by the state of Nebraska until further notice.

One of the other federal deputies did ask Longarm whether he thought they ought to wire home for a federal warrant on Sheriff Wigan, just in case he ever came back.

Longarm said, ''He'll be back. He has kin in the cattle business up this way, and it ain't as if he was telling Pronto Cross and his gang what to do. I've hashed that out with his dumb but honest deputies. I reckon Wigan was just going along with a tougher and more violent lawman gone wrong. It'll be up to the local voters, come this November, whether they want a sheriff who'd rather live and let live with bullies than stare them down. I see no serious reasons to mount a mighty expensive and uncertain federal hearing for a poor old cuss whose only crime is an unhealthy desire for peace and quiet.''

The same calm contempt applied to those other township or county officials who knew more than they'd been letting on about the Minute Men. Many, like Remington Ramsay, hadn't really known for certain just who might or might not have stuck with an officially disbanded bunch of friends and neighbors.

Leaving it to his fellow lawmen to tidy up, Longarm sent a night letter to Billy Vail in Denver, and headed back to his redecorated front room at the MacUlric boardinghouse to catch up on some well-earned rest. The new wallpaper had sunflowers against two shades of green. Longarm didn't care. He was sound asleep within seconds of his head hitting the sachet-scented pillow, and he didn't wake up until the church bells were chiming the noon hour.

He might not have opened his eyes that early had not he had to take a piss. For he had no great call to go anywhere before he'd be boarding that night train south, and that last dream had been sort of promising.

He lay there staring up at the disgustingly cheerful yellow ceiling as he muttered. ''Why is it a piss hard-on always wakes you up just as you're all set to stick it in your dream gal?''

Nobody answered. He threw the covers off, swung his bare feet to the bare planks, and considered the chamber pot under the bed. But he felt silly leaving a pot of piss where a pretty gal he'd never shown his dick to was sure to see it. So he swiftly got dressed and headed on out to do it right.

He met Mavis MacUlric in the hall, with her feather

duster. She was about the dustingest landlady he'd had in recent memory. She asked him how he liked his new wallpaper. His back teeth were floating but he had to stand there, shifting from one foot to the other, as she brought him up to date on her dawning interest in that nice Remington Ramsay.

After he'd at last been allowed to empty his bladder and tidy up the rest of him, Longarm ate dinner out back and walked Ellen Brent back to the library to say adios properly. And after she said she was never going to forget him, coming twice downstairs in the dark, she got dressed and went upstairs to open the place officially.

Longarm ambled over to the county jail, where the state troopers were set up. Longarm offered to make himself useful, but the provost sergeant said young Howard Tendring in the back had made a full confession to the attempted rape and frustrated knifing of an older gal he'd admired from afar until he hadn't been thinking straight.

Longarm said he knew the feeling. He didn't tell the older noncom who he had in mind. It was nobody's business that he'd almost managed a wet dream, and had pretended a petite brunette had been a willowy redhead just now. He asked if it was safe to assume the state troopers, since they rode for Nebraska, would see that the young killer got a fair state trial. He was assured he didn't have to worry about that mean kid any more, and so he left.

The rest of the day went as slow as a constipated cat with no place to shit. He thought more than once about riding out to the Diamond B and begging Fox Bancroft for some infernal understanding. But a gal who got sore at a man unfairly wasn't worth acting foolish over, and he knew no real gal could ever be built the way he'd pictured her in his head, whether asleep or on top of old Ellen. For being a man, he tended to picture the ones he couldn't have a bit different from the ones he could. The human mind sure teamed up with the human pecker to confound a poor innocent cuss.

But since all things good and bad must end, it only felt like a million years before Longarm was able to settle up with everyone he owed in Pawnee Junction and board that south-bound night train at last.

He rode alone in the smoking car for most of the short ride down to the main line. Ogallala, Nebraska, was a bigger cow town than the one he'd just left. But that wasn't saying much in high summer when the cows were all grazing the surrounding range and hardly anybody could afford to crowd into the bigger town's bigger whorehouses, card houses, and saloons, in that order.

Longarm got a room in one of the few hotels in Ogallala instead. The main-line day train that would carry him on to Denver wouldn't get in before breakfast time, and a man who went looking for action in a strange town late at night was a man who made more money than they paid even a senior deputy.

He carried some magazines upstairs with his light baggage, and got undressed to read himself sleepy in bed. He hadn't been reading long when there came a gentle rapping on his chamber door. So he got up to wrap a hotel towel around his waist and follow his .44-40 over to the door to see who it might be.

He hadn't really been expecting a raven. But he was surprised to see Fox Bancroft standing there in all her glory, or at least with no hat, her red hair let down, and the top buttons of her shirt neglected.

She pushed in and shut the door behind her with a boot heel as she softly said, "I don't want anyone to see me in a strange man's hotel room like this!"

To which he could only reply, lowering the muzzle of his gun at least, "Aw, I ain't so strange and to what might I owe this honor?"

She dimpled up at him in the lamplight and confided, "I was aboard the same train out of Pawnee Junction. I couldn't come forward to your smoking car because Rose Burnside was getting aboard just as I was. I waited until she'd gone to another hotel before I hired a room in this one, just down the hall.''

Longarm asked, ''How come? I thought you were sore at me about the way I had to call the shots about little Timmy and his momma.''

She seemed to be herding him backwards toward the bedstead as she said soothingly, ''I saw you had no other choice as soon as I got to thinking about it later. Rose Burnside was gushing about you on the train, by the way. She's sold out and never means to return to Pawnee Junction and its painful memories. But she's ever so grateful about the way you cleared her brother's name, and she said you spoke to her gently as well. I understand you never got fresh with Rose, or that pretty Mavis MacUlric you did so much for either.''

''Does Miss Mavis think I'm swell too?'' he asked her uncertainly. The redhead suddenly planted her shapely but work-hardened palms against his bare chest to push him hard and spill him back across the bed as she demurely replied, ''The Widow MacUlrich has her own beau. Let me tell you about the hateful man I met when my daddy sent me back East to this fancy school just before he died.''

She braced one hand against his bare chest and reached down to whip the towel from between them as she wormed a knee into his armpit on either side, saying, ''He was the leader of the debating team, and he could talk the horns off a billy goat or the pantaloons off a country girl who'd never heard such big words from a man she was in a closed carriage with! The brute seduced me when I was barely seventeen!''

Longarm gulped and said, ''I'm sure sorry you got seduced so young by a slick-talking college boy, ma'am.''

She moved a fold of her skirting out of the way as she sighed and said, ''I wasn't. It sure felt better than anything else I'd ever done. But a girl has to be so *careful*!''

He'd already risen to the occasion, and damned if she

178

didn't seem to be trying to impale her sweet self on his raging erection as he told her he had some French letters in his frock coat across the room.

Then it popped inside her and she hissed in pleasure as she settled down to take it all the way, gasping, "Don't be silly. I know how to cope with *that* worry. The *real* worry for a woman of property and some social standing is her *reputation,* and the way so many of you men carry on about your conquests! Why do you men have to crow like roosters and tell everyone for miles around that you liked it dog style?"

Longarm reached up to unbutton her denim shirt and expose nicer cupcakes than he'd pictured in his head while he told her women had been known to brag as well. So she swore she'd never tell on *him* as she whipped her skirt off over her red head.

Then he rolled her shapely form over to spread her pale thighs as wide as they could spread while he parted the red hair between them right. She moaned and begged for more as she clung to his questing shaft with her tight moist innards, and when he came in her he felt it all the way down to his toes.

For the willowy redhead combined the amorous acrobatics of the forceful Nancy from the Indian Agency with the softer submissive passion of little Ellen from that library. So a good time was had by both, and as they drifted back down through a blizzard of rose petals, he heard her murmuring, "Oh, Lord, I'd almost forgotten how swell that can feel! I never could have let myself go that way with you before I knew how considerate you'd been with Felicia Tendring, dear."

He left it in her as he protested, "Hold on. I never trifled with that murderous kid's momma! She was only acting that way with Pronto Cross to save her nasty brat! Who told you I was *this* considerate with her, damn it?"

Fox Bancroft moved her hips sensuously and purred, "Nobody. I saw for myself how you'd covered her shame for her when somebody else told me her lawyer was named Ralph! You knew all along that Uncle George was really Pronto Cross, didn't you?''

He thrust back, as any man would have, and replied, ''I was naturally on to the recorded first name of a famous town-tamer. But as you said earlier, George is a more common name than Howard. What cinched it for me was Pronto saying young Howard Tendring was a good kid when his own mother had just *told* me the town marshal had warned her about the way he'd molested that little colored gal. Felicia and her monster called him Pronto Cross in public and Uncle George around the house. I reckon he spent a heap of time around her house, after he found that a widow woman with an awful brat and a warm nature would do most anything for an understanding lawman.''

He began to thrust in time with her sensuous movements as he went on. ''There was no call for me to gossip about her and Pronto once we had him in the ground and her kid off to the lunatic asylum. She had enough to fret her heavy heart, and I doubt she or even Pronto knew the full truth before Pronto had taken the time to question little Timmy Sears closer than he let on. Once Pronto figured out what had really happened over at First Calvinist, the rest of the sad story followed as the night the day. He might not have told the real killer's mother as much as he knew. But either way, she's stuck with the simple fact that her only child is a degenerate half-wit, whilst her secret lover was a moral monster who'd murder two men, a woman, and a child just to enjoy some times like this on the sly.''

She began to move faster under him as she moaned, ''Speak for yourself, dear! I'm not sure I'd be willing to *kill* for this fine a time on the sly. But I know I'd just *die* if anyone back in Pawnee Junction knew what I was doing this very minute with the lamp lit!''

He asked her if she wanted him to trim the lamp.

She gasped, "Don't you dare stop! I only meant I couldn't be this free with any man I couldn't trust to keep my secret vices secret! I want to come this way again, and then I want to show you some *other* secret ways to have fun, you considerate sneaky thing!"

So he let her have her shocking way with him, and they never told a soul in Pawnee Junction or Denver what they'd been up to all that time in Ogallala, with the shades drawn and the lamp lit.

Watch for

LONGARM AND THE RACY LADIES

214th in the bold LONGARM series
from Jove

Coming in October!

A special offer for people who enjoy reading the best Westerns published today.

WESTERNS!

NO OBLIGATION

Mail the coupon below

To start your subscription and receive 2 FREE WESTERNS, fill out the coupon below and mail it today. We'll send your first shipment which includes 2 FREE BOOKS as soon as we receive it.